in
THE DARK

Heaven and Hell Duet

LINDSAY PAIGE

First Edition: October 2018
Library of Congress Cataloging-in-Publication Data

Paige, Lindsay
Light in the Dark (Heaven and Hell Duet) – 1st ed
ISBN-13: 978-1732587427

Stay up-to-date on books, news, sales, and giveaways by signing up for my newsletter (http://eepurl.com/hqcTw)!

And if you're a fan of the *Carolina Rebels* series, subscribers get exclusive short stories shortly after signing up!

For Perry.

Light in THE DARK

Heaven and Hell Duet

CHAPTER one

Idaline

*F*reeley Clemeth.

That's all the note from FC says. Finally, I know his name. I only came close to his first name once when I guessed Freeman. I've stared at the note every day for six months. The moment I got it, I was tempted to get in my car and drive to Raleigh. After all, that's where he is now because that's what the return address says. But the past seven months have been hell. I've had my worst bout of anxiety in years and only in the last three weeks have I pulled myself out of it a little bit.

My mind was so messed up, second guessing everything when it came to FC, and I was too chicken to even talk to him about what's been going on and the sordid thoughts I've had. He texts me every other day, still. Hoping I'm doing well and asking for a phone call. Telling me he's worried about me and if I don't talk to him soon, he's driving down here. But it's been seven months and I've yet to see him.

But today, I find myself in front of an apartment door. FC's apartment. My anxiety clutches my heart and confiscates my lungs, making it a struggle to breathe. But I didn't drive all this way to chicken out. Just as I lift my hand to knock, a voice down the hall stops me.

"He's not home."

I look toward the sound to see an elderly lady at the next apartment over.

"You're looking for FC? Who are you?" she asks skeptically.

"My name is Idaline."

The woman smiles and she hobbles over with her cane. Before I can blink, she's hugging me.

"Oh! I've heard so much about you! FC will be tickled pink to see you. He's at work, honey. I can give you the address; you should go there now. Don't wait for him here. He needs to know you've come to him." She grabs my hand and squeezes it. "What took you so long, Idaline? That boy has been waiting for you." She waves a hand in dismissal, dropping my hand. "It doesn't matter. You need to see him." She rattles off the name of a business and an address. "Go on. Put it in that phone you've got and go see my favorite neighbor."

A bit stunned, I do as she says. Fifteen minutes later, I pull in front of an automotive repair shop. Should I be disrupting FC at work? The old lady seems to think it would be okay and I'm here now anyway. With a deep breath, I walk into an office off to the side. There's a woman, who looks a bit younger than me, playing with a baby.

"Hey," she smiles. "Can I help you?"

"I'm looking for FC."

Her eyes narrow. "And you are?"

"Idaline McAllister."

Just like with the old lady, her eyes light up and she smiles. "Come on! My name is Jamie, by the way." She stands and I follow her to the shop area of the building. "FC!" she shouts. "I need you."

My heart stutters to a stop when he appears around a truck and walks this way. He doesn't see me yet. The baby goes nuts, clapping and leaning toward him. FC finally notices me. That handsome, gorgeous smile he always gave me appears.

"Idaline," he breathes. "You're here." I nod in conformation.

"I hate to spoil the moment," Jamie says, "but your son wants his daddy."

FC is distracted for a moment as he takes the little boy from her and kisses his cheek, not caring at all that he's dirty from head to toe. My brain completely stalls on what she said. His son? FC has a son? I don't understand. And he's not that little either. Maybe a year old. Oh, god. Is FC still with Lila? He's had a baby with her?

"Idaline," FC says, taking a step toward me, but that only makes me take a step back.

"Why didn't you tell me? Why did you even want me to come?" My eyes are stuck on the little boy who sucks on a pacifier and watches me with interest. "What were you expecting, FC?" I came for nothing. What a fool I am, to think I can come after he told me his name, to think we could finally be together. I swivel on my heels and haul ass out of the shop through one of the big bay doors.

"Idaline! Wait!"

I don't make it far before FC has caught up to me, grabbing my elbow. He swivels me to face him, his little boy looking a bit perplexed. God, he looks just like FC. A tiny, adorable FC.

FC wipes away one of my tears. "I need to explain everything, but I can't do that if you leave." He pulls me against his side and hugs me. "Please don't leave, Idaline," he begs with such desperation.

A tiny little hand grabs my hair and I nearly break down because I don't understand any of this.

"FC!"

FC twists.

"Take the rest of the day off. We've got it covered here."

"Are you sure?"

I lift my head in time to see a man standing near where I ran out nod.

"That's my boss, Brent. His wife is Jamie. Will you meet me at my apartment? I need to grab his stuff and then I'll be ready to go."

"Are you with Lila?" I blurt out.

FC's face turns to stone. "No. Haven't been since that Christmas before I came to see you last."

I relax at hearing that. "I'll meet you there."

Fifteen minutes later, FC and I walk into his apartment. His son rests his head on FC's shoulder, his eyelids heavy.

"What's his name?" I ask.

FC's cheeks actually redden a little. "Sawyer Nash Hart." He walks over to his couch and sits down, patting the spot next to him.

"You...you used my names." I take a seat and angle toward him, unsure how I feel about this.

"I feel like I should apologize, but I saw those names and they were it for me." He rocks side to side a little, slowly rocking his son to sleep. "That night I left you? The last time I saw you? Lila went into labor. He wasn't due until March, but he came into the world perfect and beautiful anyway," he says, glancing down at Sawyer. "The moment I got full custody of him, I moved back to Raleigh and once I was settled in here with him, I sent you the note with my name on it."

"So, he's what you were keeping from me? How did you end up with full custody? Did Lila move here too?" There are so many questions and he can't answer them soon enough.

"Not entirely," FC says, looking back up at me. He sighs and leans his head back, looking up at the ceiling. "All those bruises I had? When my back was hurt? They were from Lila. She would hit me. That's what I didn't want to tell you. I only told my parents when I found out she was pregnant." And I continue to listen as FC tells me the horrors of his relationship with Lila. How she abused him. How she essentially got pregnant on purpose. How she kept tempting him to relapse. How she used a damn *whip* to beat him. And then, he tells me how she was once Sawyer was born and how she suddenly gave up her rights.

"I haven't let my guard down yet," he tells me. "She wouldn't do that for nothing, Idaline, and I'm sure she'll come after me and Sawyer at some point. That's every-thing I didn't want to tell you. It's embarrassing and I felt like it would be easier to explain once I was out of the sit-uation than while I was still in it. And I didn't want you worrying about me either. I'm sorry, Idaline, I really am, but that's the only way I could handle it."

"Why didn't you leave her?" I ask.

"Once she was pregnant, I didn't feel like I could. I didn't trust her to take care of Sawyer or herself. She even smoked a few times because she knew I went to see you and that was her way of getting me to do what she wanted. Before that, I was too embarrassed and ashamed."

This is so much information to process. "And what do you want now that I'm here? What were you expecting?"

"Us to be together," he replies simply. "If that's what you want."

My eyes drift to the little boy, who sleeps soundly now. I'd love nothing more than to be with FC, but he's asking so much of me. I wasn't expecting a one-year-old. That's a lot to add on to a potential relationship, and I'm not sure if I can handle it, or if I'm prepared for it.

"It's a lot to ask, I know," he says, echoing my thoughts, "and I don't expect an answer anytime soon. But you're all caught up on my life now; you can make which-ever decision is best for you." He takes a deep breath. "What's been going on with you? You disappeared on me."

"It's been a bad time with my anxiety," I answer. "I waited until I was in a better place to come see you. You really fucked with my head, FC." He frowns, but I push through. "You had this big secret and you ran out on me the morning after we first had sex. Everything kept getting worse and worse in my head and my anxiety had a field day. It took me forever to get myself back to as normal as can be. And now," I shake my head, "I never could've imagined this."

"Idaline," he says in his soft, heartbreaking tone like I've crushed his soul. "Come here," he whispers. FC lifts his arm and I snuggle against his side, but that causes his son to take up most of my line of vision. "We're soulmates, remember? We'll get this all worked out."

"I don't know if it'll be that simple, FC."

"It never is, love. Nothing about us has been simple; I don't expect any different now that there's a potential for us to be together." He kisses my head. "Why don't you relax here for a bit? I'm going to lay him down and take a shower, get cleaned up. How long are you here for?"

I sit up and shrug. "I wasn't really expecting to come today. I just packed a bunch of clothes and told my work I needed to take off for a while." I leave out the part where they fired me because it was so last-minute. They threatened to do it, but I didn't care anymore. Coming here was exactly what I needed to do. I'll worry about everything else later.

"Will you stay tonight?" he asks hopefully.

I nod. It's a long drive back home and I'm not ready to leave yet.

FC gets up and disappears on me to do as he planned: laying Sawyer down and to take his shower. My mind is a whirlwind while he's gone, never focusing on one thing for too long. How could all those things happen to him and I not connect the dots? How did I not realize he was being abused? How difficult it must have been to keep that to himself. And then to add a baby to the mix? I can't imagine.

My worst fear comes to life when I hear a wail from one of the bedrooms FC disappeared to first. After panicking for two seconds, in which FC doesn't leave his bedroom, I get up and walk to Sawyer's room.

He stands in his crib, crying, stopping when he sees me.

"Hey, Sawyer," I say softly as I slowly approach him. "Your daddy isn't available at the moment, so I'm all you've got."

"DaDa," he hiccups.

What am I supposed to do with this kid? I've never been around kids. Not that much, at least. And as a nurse, I worked mostly with elderly folks. The closer I get to Sawyer, he lifts his arms. He wants me to pick him up? He doesn't even know me!

With a deep, shaky breath, I pick him up and rest him on my hip. Sawyer stares at me, both of us wondering what's next. A door creaks and we swivel. Thank goodness. FC appears in the doorway, wearing only a towel around his waist.

"I thought I heard him. Are you okay, Idaline?"

"I feel out of my element."

He smiles easily. "Come sit in here." FC grabs a nearby book and I follow him into his bedroom. My eyes stick on his back and all the scars there. My heart breaks, thinking about the pain he endured for so long due to such a hateful woman. He directs me to sit on his bed, handing Sawyer the book, which makes a crinkling sound with his every touch. "Shout if you need me," FC says before he disappears into his bathroom.

Sawyer holds the book up to me.

"Do you want me to read to you?" I ask.

He pushes the tiny book closer to my face, so I take it and read it. It's not very entertaining. It's a counting book with animals and it only goes up to five. When I finish, Sawyer looks at me expectantly, so I begin again. This time, I add the noises the animals make. Mostly to make it more appealing to myself, but Sawyer giggles and claps, so he's enjoying it too. By the end of the third read, I also get an ovation from FC.

He grins from his stance by the door frame. "We'll be fine, Idaline."

I'm still not so sure.

FC walks over and takes Sawyer from me. "Sawyer, this is Idaline." He points to me. "Can you say Idaline?" Sawyer puts his book in his mouth instead, causing FC to laugh. "We'll try again another time, son." Watching FC kiss his forehead is ridiculously sweet. FC holds out his hand, which I take, and we leave his bedroom. "He didn't sleep as long as I thought he would. His afternoon naps are at least an hour." FC sits on the floor with Sawyer, dragging a basket of toys close to them. "He may get cranky at some point." FC pats the space next to him and waits for me to take my seat.

I, of course, sit down as expected. "He looks so much like you."

FC smiles and I swear his chest swells with pride. "Best compliment ever."

Sawyer goes from toy to toy before standing and walking around the couch. When he seems to head toward the hallway, FC chuckles softly. "Son?" Sawyer turns around. "Where do you think you're going? Get back over here." He waves a toy in the air, but Sawyer laughs and takes his little legs wobbling faster down the hall. FC laughs and runs after him.

The squeal and peal of laughter lets me know Sawyer was caught. Sawyer hangs down FC's back when they re-appear. "I'm going to eat your feet since you ran away," FC threatens right before he nibbles and tickles his feet with his free hand. Sawyer laughs, and it's such a beautiful little laugh. "You better ask Idaline to help you." FC winks before turning so Sawyer can see me. "Tell her. Say help. Help!"

He does talk, but nothing comes out sounding like help.

I laugh, stand, and go over. Sawyer holds his arms out and I grab him. "I'll save you." FC releases his hold once he realizes I have him. He whirls around and I twist my chest to keep Sawyer away.

I don't even have to encourage him before he says, "DaDa!" and a bunch of other nonsense when FC holds his hands up as if he's about to issue a tickle assault.

"No? Are you sure you don't want the tickle monster to come see you? Maybe Idaline does?" His grin is wicked.

"FC, I'm holding your son," I remind him.

He rolls his eyes. "Fine." He holds out his arms for Sawyer, who eyes him with suspicion. "Let's play." Those must be the magic words because he leans toward FC with that.

We return to the floor and do our best to entertain Sawyer.

CHAPTER Two

FC

I glance over at Idaline, who seems a bit lost. She stares down at her hands. It's as if she's zoned out on us and doesn't even hear all the noise Sawyer makes right now. I reach over and take her hand, startling her.

"You okay?"

"It's a bit overwhelming," she admits with a small smile.

That is understandable. "Do you need some time to yourself? You can go in my room and get away from all of this," I motion to the rug covered with toys and my son who bangs two of them together, "if you need to for as long as you'd like."

Her eyes tell me she really wants to do this, but she hesitates for some reason.

"Idaline, it's been a long, information-packed day. Add a kid to that and you're bound to be exhausted. And if you're still having anxiety issues, you really need the break, I'm guessing. Go take it. We'll be fine. The only one required to be around Sawyer right now is me. If you need to take a breather, love, take it. We won't mind."

She leans over and kisses me quickly. "Thank you," she whispers.

My eyes trail after her, lingering on the subtle sway of her hips as she walks until Sawyer gets my attention in a terrible way. One of the worst things about babies is when they try to stand and use you to do it. That doesn't sound so bad, right? But what if you had long arm hair and they like to pull at it? Sawyer does that shit when he uses my arm to pull himself up to stand or when he's not paying attention and just grabs my arm. He's yanked at my arm hairs so much, I'm surprised I have any hair left.

"Let's settled down some, son. Want to help me cook? Are you hungry?" I tickle his stomach, causing him to laugh. "Nom nom nom?" I ask. That's another way of me asking him if he wants to eat.

"Nom!" he grunts back. The two words he clearly knows are DaDa and nom.

I grab something for him to play with before sitting him in his highchair while I go about getting our dinner together. Before I can grab anything out of the fridge, there's a knock on my door. I pick Sawyer up and take him with me to answer it.

There on the other side is my mother.

"I brought dinner," she announces, handing me the bag and reaching for Sawyer all in one swift move that has been done plenty of times.

"Enough for a plus one if I have one?" I ask as she walks past me.

"What are you talking about?"

"Idaline's here."

Mom twists and turns, looking for her. "Here?"

"She needed a break, so she's in my room."

"Wow."

We get Sawyer back in his highchair. Mom always brings too much food, so there's plenty for Idaline, too. Mom feeds Sawyer while I lean against the fridge.

"How is it going?"

I shrug. "She's more thrown off by Sawyer than anything else, I think."

Mom nods. "You can't expect her to come in and be Sawyer's mom."

"I don't," I interrupt. "Would it be great if she eventually took that role? Yeah, sure, but we're nowhere near that happening."

"But she knows that's what it'll be and she might not be ready for that so soon anyway," Mom points out. "She came here, thinking she was getting you. And now, she finds out she's getting you and a little boy. That's a lot for a woman. It's not even her son."

"Mom," I chastise. "I may not know everything about Idaline, but I know enough that the most important thing to her about Sawyer is that he's a part of me. I know it's a lot to put on her, but it's not like I won't give her whatever time she may need, too. She's the one I need to be with and I'll do everything to make it happen."

"What if she doesn't want kids?" Mom asks point blank.

"She does." Otherwise, she wouldn't keep a list of favorite names for potential kids.

"What if right now in her life, she doesn't want to date someone with a baby?"

That's the question, isn't it? Maybe since she's still here, that means it's not a dealbreaker for her. I don't know. All I know is I need Idaline and she needs me. Sawyer scares her and that's my fault for not preparing her at all for the fact that he exists. All I need to do is make her see that we can make this work. She can handle this. We're soulmates. That's what she said. She can't give up on me now.

"Can I stay and meet her?" Mom asks later when I'm giving Sawyer his bath. When I peeked on Idaline earlier, she was asleep and I haven't bothered waking her up.

"No. I'd rather you go on and leave. I've overwhelmed her enough for one day." When Mom sighs, I add, "When she's ready, you can. I'm not rushing Idaline."

"Rushing me how?"

I twist, making sure my hold is firm on Sawyer, and see Idaline standing behind my mother in the doorway of the bathroom. "Rushing you to meet my parents," I answer. "Idaline, this is my mother, Jennifer. Mom, this is Idaline. Mom was just leaving."

They exchange pleasantries, which is fine, until I hear my mom ask, "You don't mind if I stay for a few minutes to chat with you, do you, Idaline?"

"Uh," Idaline falters.

"Mom!" I snap harshly, startling poor Sawyer. He looks at me with wide eyes. "Sorry, buddy," I apologize to him. "You heard what I said, Mom. Go home."

She wiggles past me to kiss the top of Sawyer's head, squeezes my shoulder, and says goodbye to Idaline on her way out. A moment later, Idaline kneels next to me.

"Was that necessary?" she asks softly as Sawyer goes back to kicking his legs and splashing water, his favorite thing to do.

"I told her I didn't want you meeting them yet because I put enough on you already. It wasn't right for her to put you on the spot like that. So, yes, it was necessary."

She's quiet for a moment before she rests her head on my shoulder. "So, I guess it's okay for me to be glad you did that?"

I laugh. "Yeah, it's okay. Do you feel better?"

"Yeah."

"Good. I've already got him all clean, but I let him play for a bit afterward. He loves it so much. I can't wait to take him to the pool or the beach." Sawyer picks up a cup full of water, dumps it on his head, and looks at me while he belly laughs. "If only he loved baths this much when he was a tiny little thing. He would scream his lungs out until I put clothes back on him. It was the most stressful experience ever with him."

Sawyer holds the cup out to me, so I do the same thing to him.

"You've been taking care of him all by yourself?" Idaline asks.

"My family helps if I need it, but otherwise, yeah. Pretty much since the day he was born. Lila didn't have much to do with him before she gave up her rights."

"I don't understand how she could walk away from him. I mean, I know I'm having some anxiety about this whole thing, but this is her son. She carried him and gave birth to him. How does she not care for him?" She looks at me for the answer and I give her one.

"Because she's heartless."

With that, I drain the water and take Sawyer out to dry and clothe him. Afterward, I pick out a book and return to the living room where Idaline sits. The moment I sit in the recliner, Sawyer cuddles up to my side, crossing his feet at his ankles. We gently rock while I read the book to him. This is our nightly routine and always has been. He'll be asleep in no time.

And within ten minutes, I've placed him in his bed, returned his book to its shelf, and come to sit next to Idaline.

"I know that you told me all I had to do was wait for your secret, but I still feel like you've betrayed me somehow. This seems too big, at least with Sawyer. If you didn't want to tell me about Lila yet, fine, but you should've told me about Sawyer, FC."

"I'm sorry," I say. "I can't change it now and I handled it in the way I thought was best, even though I knew there would be consequences."

She rests her head on my shoulder and takes my hand in hers. "What were you expecting?"

"For you to be upset at first, but then we'd reconnect and start on this journey together. I don't expect it to be as easy as it sounds, but as long as you're here and we try, I think we'll work out." When she doesn't say anything, I add, "We can visit one another, get the hang of being in a relationship together, and once you're ready, you can move here." At that, she looks up at me. "I don't want to take Sawyer away from my family."

"I can't believe we're even talking about this," she says, a touch of awe in her voice, as she shakes her head.

I smile. A part of me can't believe it either. "Tell me a secret," I request.

Her mood dives off a cliff with whatever she thinks of first. "I was fired this morning."

"What? Why?"

"I didn't give advance notice for my vacation and I didn't care about their very real threats. I needed to come see you today. Not tomorrow. Not next week. Not a month from now. I'm not worried about it right now, but I'm sure it'll hit me soon and I'll have a panic attack about the fact that I have zero income coming in."

Oh, my Idaline. This is not good news. She doesn't give me a chance to comment on this development because she asks for a secret in return. What I want to say comes rather quickly. "Sometimes, I look at Sawyer and feel nothing but guilt." I've been dying to share this secret with her for ages and now, I can. It's not a nice, pretty secret, but it's a real one and it'll do for our purposes.

Idaline sits up and looks at me. "Why?"

"I didn't want him." Her eyes widen as a small gasp escapes. "I thought I would be trapped with Lila for the rest of my life with a baby she made sure she got pregnant with. So, no, I didn't want him. There was nothing but negative feelings toward him. But from the second he was born, I fell in love with him. So, sometimes, I look at him and I remember how I felt and I can't believe I ever felt that way. It makes me feel guilty."

Her eyes are so sad, which makes me wish I hadn't told her this secret. "I'm sorry, FC. But it's obvious you love and care for him; that means more now than how you felt before he was born."

"Maybe," I say, not wanting to fully agree. The guilt won't allow me to do so.

"Can we go to bed?" she asks.

Like I'd ever say no to that. Idaline stays in my apartment, just in case Sawyer wakes up, while I venture down to her car to grab her bags. My heart feels even more at peace than usual. Idaline will soon fall asleep in my arms in my bed. There's nothing else I could ask for today.

Back inside, my gaze constantly lands on Idaline as we prepare for bed, as if I need to repeatedly check that she is indeed here with me. Seconds after we crawl beneath the sheets, our bodies find their way to one another. Our arms wrap around each other's waists. Our chests collide.

"What if I move here now? I can start looking for a place tomorrow and a new job," Idaline whispers.

While this sounds fantastic to me, I worry Idaline isn't actually ready. Is she making this decision out of anxiety somehow? Or is this really what she wants to do? And how can I ask without pissing her off?

"FC?"

"Are you sure that's truly what you want? We don't have to rush." There. I put it out there the best way I can.

"If we're going to make this work, I don't want this to be long distance. I don't want to go back home. Things have been hard enough as it is; why make it any harder on myself? I can't do it, FC. I can't go home. I can't leave you and do this all over again. It's now or never and I need you now. This can't be prolonged any more."

Hearing her distress is almost too much to handle. There is no argument to be made, not that I could even think of one to make. "If you want to move here, you won't get anything but support from me," I tell her.

She kisses me quickly. "Thank you, Freeley."

I groan, which makes her laugh. "Don't call me that, Idaline."

"It does sound odd when you've always been FC to me. I still couldn't resist, though."

She settles in, scooting a hair closer to me, and tells me goodnight before dozing off. This is the moment I've been dreaming of for over a year now. It's better than I could've imagined. And to think that Idaline will be moving here and we'll be together? Pure bliss runs through my veins.

Complete happiness is at the tips of my fingers and now that Idaline is here, I know it'll be fully in my grasp soon.

CHAPTER Three

Idaline

A soft kiss wakes me up. "Sorry, love, but I need you to wake up." I smile just because he's calling me *love*. "And we need to talk a few things over."

I stretch and open my eyes, a bit startled to find him already dressed for work and Sawyer in his lap, quietly playing with a toy. "What's up?"

"My mom will be over soon to keep Sawyer for me today, and then I have to leave for work. Will you be okay here with her? Or you could come and hang out with Jamie? I would feel better if you came with me." He tickles Sawyer a bit. "I don't want Mom pressuring you all day. I'm sure you could take your laptop and look for jobs and such from the shop."

"I'll go with you if that's what you want."

FC gives me one of his breathtaking smiles. I get ready and finish just in time to leave with FC. My decision was the right one because the look his mother gives me is definitely one that wishes to crack me open and discover all my darkest secrets.

My heart and mind already feel better than they did yesterday. It's all for the simple fact that FC is near. My soul entwines with his and sighs with contentment, finally in its paradise. My heart dances to a happier beat and my mind relaxes knowing that whatever battles I'll face, FC is here to face them with me.

"How are you feeling today?" he asks, pointing to his head.

"Good, but starting to worry about not having a job."

FC reaches over to hold my hand. "Don't worry about that. You'll start looking today and you'll find something soon."

When he lifts our joined hands, I ache to tell him I love him. Three powerful words I've wanted to say for such a long time, yet this morning doesn't seem like the time to utter them. FC escorts me to the main office, where Jamie already sits behind her desk. She perks up at seeing me.

"Do I have a visitor today?" she asks.

"If it's okay with you and Brent?"

She waves her hand in dismissal. "Brent won't care. Let me grab you a seat and you can sit back here with me."

As Jamie sets about doing that, FC turns to me. "Come find me if you need me; otherwise, I'll see you at lunch. You're in good hands with Jamie." My heart slows to a stop as he leans forward and kisses me softly on the mouth. The *I love you* is on the tip of my tongue once more.

"Okay, FC. Go work before I report to the boss that you're wasting time in my office," Jamie says. "I'll be nice to Idaline, I promise."

FC squeezes my hand before disappearing into the shop. Jamie ushers me into the chair she brought around.

She eyes me as if I'm a long-lost toy or something. "FC's in love with you, you know. He hadn't worked here for a week before everyone in the shop knew about you and how he was essentially waiting for you. That's why you're here, isn't it?"

Well, she jumps right to the point and doesn't beat around the bush at all.

"Yes," I answer.

Jamie grins. "That's awesome to hear. I promise that's as much as I'll get into your business. I do my best to stay out of other people's lives, but I had to get that much out. If you need a friend, I'm an option. I know you're new to the area and it can't hurt to have someone close by other than FC to talk to, if needed."

"Thanks."

For the first two hours, in between interruptions from phone calls and customers coming in, Jamie and I get to know one another better. She seems like a pretty cool person. She could easily become a friend of mine. Once she declares she must actually focus on work, she gives me the wifi password and I'm able to focus on some of my list of things to do as well.

I figure I better look for a job first. It won't do me much good to get an apartment if I don't have income coming in. There are a few positions available in the area and I spend every moment until FC comes to find me for lunch filling out applications. One of them has to pan out.

"How was your morning?" FC asks as we leave for lunch.

"Good. Jamie is nice and I've been filling out job applications all morning. I'll hunt for an apartment when I get back."

"Are you still feeling good about moving here? No second thoughts or hesitations?" FC glances at me as he stops at a stoplight.

Honestly, I feel lighter than I have in months. It's as if my mentality needed a change of scenery. A fresh start to erase the bad feelings and anxieties, and that's moving close to FC and officially starting a relationship with him. "This feels like the best decision I've made in a long time," I tell him, causing him to grin as the light turns green.

We soon arrive at a restaurant. FC takes my hand, but we don't speak until after we've placed our orders. FC looks a bit hesitant, nervous, and I worry about what he'll say.

"You're," he takes a deep breath. "You're okay with not moving in with me, right? I mean, I'd love to someday, but don't you think it's too soon? And with Sawyer involved, I don't want to rush anything, especially since I threw you for a loop where he is involved."

"FC," I interrupt because it seems as if he wants to keep on talking. "It's fine. I don't want to move in with you right now. Maybe someday, like you said. I think it'll be too much too soon for us to take that step. I want my own place." Not only do I think it's too soon for us, but I still want my own space for when I may need it, anxiety-wise.

FC relaxes. "Okay, good. I'm glad we're on the same page then. Can I take you on a proper date tonight?"

"I don't have any other plans," I tease with a laugh.

He smiles and lifts my hand to his mouth for a kiss. "Then you're all mine as long as Sawyer has a babysitter."

This feels so surreal. Not only that I'm here with FC, but that after all this time, we're talking about going on dates. Talking about relationships and moving closer to one another so we can be together like we've always wanted.

"What's the smile for?" FC asks.

I didn't even realize I was smiling. "I'm glad I'm here is all." Not much can bring me down from this high.

We spend more time catching up over lunch before returning to FC's work. There, I search for places to rent and make appointments for later in the week to look at a few different places. FC buzzes with energy on the way home, knowing we'll have our first date tonight.

His mom heads home soon after we arrive, as his nana is actually the one who will babysit for him. I'm both nervous and a bit excited about meeting her. I play with Sawyer on FC's bed while FC showers. It's not as hard or complicated as I thought it might be to keep the baby oc-cupied. He likes playing with the toys FC left him and it seems easy to find ways to entertain him.

When he leans against my chest while he plays with a stuffed animal, an odd feeling wraps around my soul. It's such a sweet action. It's as if he's comfortable with me already, even though I don't feel as if I'm fully there yet with him.

"Do you even know who I am?" I ask him like he might answer.

Sawyer looks up at me.

"Idaline. Can you say that? I-da-line." I repeat it a few more times while he says words he understands and tosses in a few DaDas, but eventually, he swoops in and steals my heart.

"AhDa," he says.

I smile, earning one from him, and clap my hands, which causes him to do the same. "That's it! Good job, Sawyer. AhDa," I repeat, hoping to hear him say it again.

"AhDa!"

Oh, I think I love this little boy a little bit. "Can you say your name? Saw-yer. Sawyer. Try it. Sawyer."

"I love you with him."

I snap my head up to look at FC, standing in the doorway between his bedroom and his bathroom, with only a towel wrapped around his waist. All I can do right now is stare and hope I'm not drooling.

"He's pretty smitten with you already." He nods to where Sawyer still rests against my chest.

"I have to say, I'm a little smitten myself. He's so sweet and cute."

FC blows me away with his smile. There's a loud knock on the door. "That must be Nana. Let me let her in and then I'll get dressed." I pick up Sawyer and follow him. My eyes can't help but stare at his scars once more.

He opens the door, but it's not his nana. I know this in one glance for a few reasons. One, the woman on the other side isn't old. She's young, maybe around our age or so. She has a black eye and a gash along her nose. FC's entire body goes rigid the moment he sees her.

Her eyes leave FC and land on me. "Who is that bitch with my son?"

Oh, god. This is Lila.

FC fills the doorway with his body, blocking her view from us, and something makes me disappear far enough down the hallway to be hidden from view, just in case. "You need to leave, Lila. There's a restraining order still in place and you have no right to be here."

"FC, babe, I miss you."

"Leave, Lila. You have ten seconds to walk away before I call the law to remove you. There's no reason at all to be here and less reason when I add in the fact that there's a restraining order."

"I want to see my son."

"You don't have a son," he corrects her, his voice hard and harsh, making me flinch.

"Babe."

I hear a slap. "Get your fucking hands off me. My babysitter is calling the law right now." Does he mean me? I hurry to his bedroom to grab his phone. Sawyer whines a little and clings to my neck. As I walk back down the hallway, I hear the door slam closed. When I peer around into the living room, FC paces.

"Is everything okay?" I ask.

FC whirls around. He stalks toward me and nearly snatches Sawyer from my hold. "We're not going out tonight. I need to make some phone calls." He takes his phone as well and returns to the door, constantly peering out the peephole. He yanks the door open and then pulls an elderly lady inside.

"Boy, don't you manhandle me like that!" she chides.

"Did you pass a car on the way in?"

"No," she answers with confusion.

"Fuck," he mutters.

"What's this about, FC?"

"Lila was just here. If you didn't pass a car on its way out, then she might still be in the parking lot."

Her eyes widen. "That hussy is here?" She turns. "Let me go find her."

Just as she opens the door again, FC pushes it closed. "Nana, I don't think you're equipped to go after Lila. Just take Sawyer and let me call Karen, see if she knows why in the fuck that woman is back in my life."

When his nana takes Sawyer is when she notices me. "Oh my. Idaline. Please forgive me, dear. Hello." She advances toward me for a hug. "It's nice to meet you. I apologize that it's when a messy situation has unfolded. Come with me. Let's give FC a moment alone."

She pulls a reluctant me away and down to Sawyer's room. "Can you tell me what happened?"

"He opened the door, thinking it was you. She asked who was holding her baby. He kept telling her she needed to leave because of a restraining order. She said she missed him. He had to threaten to call the law. That's pretty much it. Oh. She had a black eye and a gash on her face."

His nana's eyes light up and she blows my mind with a chuckle. "Sounds like someone finally gave her what she was dishing out."

"Fuck!" FC shouts, startling Sawyer enough that he cries.

"Go check on him will you, dear?" she asks as she rocks Sawyer.

I take the opportunity to get away from the crying baby, who surprisingly makes me nervous. FC paces around the living room, but stops when he sees me.

"She's fucking crazy," he says. "Her mom said she was able to convince her to give up her rights in the first place because it would be Lila's way of showing me she cared enough about Sawyer to put him first. But Lila got a new boyfriend and when that didn't pan out because he's as bad as she is, she thought she'd come back to me and I'd accept her since she proved how much she loved my son by giving him up."

This FC is the same one who would come to my apartment because he needed to get away from Lila. He's tense, irritated, and no happiness can be found. My heart and soul ache at seeing him like this, especially compared to how happy he was only a short while ago. I walk over and hug him, stopping him from his pacing. His arms dangle down by his sides for a few seconds before he hugs me back.

"This is not how our new relationship is supposed to go," he whispers, hugging me tighter. "I'm sorry we're not going out tonight, but I don't want to leave him with her out there somewhere." He pauses. "Fuck, I need a drink."

"What you need is this hug. And don't worry about it," I tell him. "She can't be that much of a problem when you've already won. Sawyer is yours; there's nothing she can do about that now. You have a restraining order, so if she violates it again, all you have to do is report her and she'll get in trouble."

"Problem is I don't want to deal with her at all. She's supposed to be out of our lives." His voice is tortured and troubled once again; I hate hearing it. "One reason I waited until she was gone to tell you about everything was because I didn't want the entire situation stressing you out. To add any anxiety on you, and now she's back." He sighs heavily.

"I'll be okay, FC."

He pulls back to look at me, pushing my hair behind my ear. "You're telling me your heart isn't going nuts?" He places a hand over my chest, which confirms on his own that he's correct. "You've been having a hard time lately; I don't want to add to that. I don't want to make it worse. Your mental health is too important."

"But do you know what's just as important?" I ask. His brows raise in question. "Us. Being together. I don't want anything to stand in our way again. We're stronger than that, FC. We've only just begun; don't think of cutting me loose."

His arms tighten around me. "I'm not," he vehemently swears. "I'm just worried."

That's understandable.

"Everything okay in here?"

We turn to face Nana who holds Sawyer's hand. He pulls away from her and walks as fast as he can over to FC, who picks him up and hugs him as if he hasn't seen him in months.

"It will be," FC says.

"I'll start dinner. Are you still staying or do you want to go out?"

"We're not going anywhere. And you don't have to cook, Nana."

She waves him off and starts for the kitchen. FC shakes his head with a smile, disappears to his room to get dressed before returning, and sits down on the floor with Sawyer. Do I stay with FC or help Nana? Instinctively feeling as if FC needs some time with Sawyer, I head to the kitchen.

Nana immediately orders me around, for which I'm thankful. It's better to get orders than to awkwardly stand around and wonder what to help with or to ask. While we're working together, she asks me questions.

"I'm glad you're here, Idaline," she says quietly, as if she doesn't want FC to overhear. "Do you two have a game plan to make this relationship work? Because if I know FC, there will definitely be a relationship with you. He's waited too long to be with you not to."

My heart warms at hearing such things, even though FC essentially told me the same thing. "I'm moving here. It'll be official once I can find a job and an apartment in order to move my things here."

She smiles. "Good. I'm available any time you two want to go out for a date. I love my grandson and my great-grandson. What does your family think about all of this?"

At this, I glance away. My family doesn't know I'm here. Not even my grandpa. It was that much of an impulsive decision to come for FC.

"Idaline?" Nana pushes. "Please tell me someone knows you're here, dear."

"Idaline?" I swivel around to face FC. "Your folks don't know you're here?" His face bunches into a frown. "Why?"

My gaze flicks between his worried and upset stare to Nana's curious one. What am I supposed to say? "I'll tell them eventually," I find myself saying.

FC's frown deepens. "When? When Grandpa McAllister shows up and discovers you're not home and haven't been? I don't need to give him any more reason to dislike me. Why haven't you told them?" he repeats.

Anxiety buds, grows, and festers in my chest. My fingertips tingle and my breathing increases. FC closes the distance between us to hold my face in his hands. That lone action causes me to spill. "They'll worry. They might not like it. I don't need to deal with anything but support and what if they don't give it to me?"

He kisses my forehead. "You can't quietly move away without anyone knowing, love. They'll worry more. Tell the person who will be the most understanding so at least one person knows."

"DaDa!" Sawyer shouts, suddenly appearing next to us while babbling. "Nom!"

FC laughs. "We're working on dinner, son. Give us some time," he says as he picks Sawyer up. When his gaze returns to me, he says, "Go call someone, please. It'll be fine, I promise."

With my heart down by my feet, I leave everyone in the kitchen to walk down to FC's bedroom to call my grandpa. I should probably call my parents, but my gut tells me to call him instead.

"Idaline, how are you?" he answers. "Shouldn't you be at work?"

"Um, fine. You?"

There's a pause and then, "What's going on, Idaline? You sound nervous. Do I need to come over for us to talk?"

"No," I quickly squeak.

"Tell me," he demands while I mentally curse myself for being so obvious.

"I'm in North Carolina." My grandpa sighs, but I push forward. "I'm moving here to be with him."

"Oh, Idaline," he sighs.

"I need support, Grandpa," I plead. "I want you to tell everyone else. This is where I need to be. I'm already happier here and I've been here since yesterday."

Grandpa is silent for a second before he says, "Tell me everything that's been going on. You have my support, and I'll handle things here. If you need help moving, I'll help you. But I need to properly meet this boy and his family."

So, I tell him about everything that's happened and all I've learned since being here. More anxiety chips away at knowing my grandpa is in my corner and he'll handle things back home for me.

CHAPTER Four

FC

"That girl is troubled, FC," Nana says as we sit down to eat.

I frown. "She's not trouble."

She rolls her eyes. "That's not what I said. She's troubl*ed*."

My gaze shifts toward the hallway. Idaline is still in the bedroom, talking to her grandfather. It doesn't bring me much comfort that Nana can sense Idaline isn't her complete self, too. "She'll be all right," I say as both a reassurance to her and myself.

Sawyer talks as we eat until a few minutes later, Idaline emerges looking way more relaxed than she has been. Grandpa McAllister pulled through.

"Everything go well?" I ask anyway as she takes a seat next to me, her plate already full and waiting.

"Yes," she replies with a smile. "I feel much better."

LIGHT IN THE DARK

"Good."

Dinner goes easy while Nana and Idaline talk, learning about one another and laughing over my childhood antics. If I let myself, I could forget that Lila showed up. But that's an impossibility at this moment. What I do instead is focus every thought and sight on Idaline and Sawyer. They are the two most important people right now.

Nana leaves shortly after dinner, making me promise she can babysit for us tomorrow. Idaline stays in the living room while I set about giving Sawyer a bath, letting him play until he's pruny, and then reading to him until he falls asleep.

Once he's down for the count, I return to the living room and sit down on the couch next to Idaline. A sigh of happiness leaves me as she leans into my side, getting comfortable. She takes my hand in hers, holding it in her lap.

"I've missed this so much. Being near you and having my heart beat crazily wondering what might happen next," she says softly.

"We haven't had nearly enough time together. Are you sure you've missed it?" I tease.

She looks up at me, completely serious. "Definitely."

I expect her to rest her head on my shoulder again, but her gaze doesn't move away from mine. The world slips away the longer we stare. My eyes drop to her lips when her tongue peeks out to swipe across her lower lip. Our breathing shallows at the same time.

"Mind if I kiss you?" I'm not sure why exactly I'm asking or why I feel like I should, but I do all the same.

Idaline smiles. "Please do."

Our mouths join quite simply. Just a closing of the distance in order to make contact. One chaste kiss before our mouths open and our tongues war, chase, and caress one another. Idaline's soft moan goes straight to my dick. She grabs ahold of my neck as if she needs to keep me right where I am. Like I would go anywhere. She tastes better than I remember, feels better as my hands glide up and down her body, and smells just as sweet.

Five minutes into this kissing, Idaline moves swiftly until she straddles my lap. Such a bad idea that I love so much. My hips immediately jerk up to rub against her. God, she moans again as she presses down against my hips, like we're two teenagers who aren't allowed to go any further than this right here.

My body aches when Idaline suddenly pulls away.

"Are you okay?" I ask, hoping I haven't somehow fucked up.

She nods. "Is it too soon for us to have sex?" Her nervousness sneaks out in her question.

My answer is obviously no. "That's for you to decide, love. If you're ready, I'm ready. If you're not, there's no harm done in waiting. There is zero pressure from me; you know that, right?"

"Yes," she answers resolutely. "I would just like that connection with you." Her fingers walk their way down my chest, slip underneath my T-shirt, and her hands flatten as they slide back up. "Sometimes, our last night together feels like nothing more than a dream. And I'm left wondering if we were really together or not. Did I really remember how you felt or was I imagining things?" Her head tilts to the side as her hips rock against me. Her breath hitches while her nails dig into my skin. Finally, her eyes lift to mine. "You don't understand how much I've missed you. How much I've always wanted to be with you."

She has no idea. I run my hands up her back until I reach her shoulders and then pull her into a tight hug. "I understand perfectly, Idaline. You've always been the light in my dark world, always unreachable, unattainable, but now you're here and I don't plan on ever letting you go. On ever letting you down or to allow the dark to take over my world again." Lila can show up all she wants, but nothing will stand in the way of my happiness and all the potential happiness I'll have with Idaline ever again.

Idaline looks at me with water in her eyes. "I love you," she whispers.

My chest swells, air stays locked in my lungs for a solid moment, and I smile. This is the first time she's ever said those words. I've felt love from her, but to hear her say it and to know she doesn't mean it in a strict friendship sense? It's the highest of highs. Especially since I never expected her to say it to me first. With a good solid hold on her, moving my hands to her legs, I stand.

Silently, I walk to my bedroom with her in my arms. Idaline has the slightest of frowns on her face, but I'll erase that in just a moment. She releases me the second I set her on the edge of the bed and loses all contact with me.

"Idaline?"

"Yeah?"

I lift her chin to make her look at me. There's unnecessary worry in her eyes. "I love you too."

LINDSAY PAIGE

The moment the words are out of my mouth, she pulls me in for a kiss and frantically goes about undressing me. That moment was fourteen years in the making. The only thing I can promise, with words and actions, is that it won't take another fourteen years to solidify the fact that we'll spend the rest of our lives together.

Waking up with a naked Idaline wrapped around my body. Is there anything better than that? Not really. I softly kiss her forehead and carefully extract myself so I can shower before Sawyer wakes up. While last night was one of the most amazing in my life, I can't help but think about how it's a new day and that means new problems.

Did Lila head back home or is she still lurking around?

My gut tells me she's still lurking around.

Which means I need as many eyes as possible on Sawyer today. I don't know how crazy she may get and I don't want to risk anything happening to him. Although, again, my gut tells me she has no concern for Sawyer. She isn't here for him. She's here for me.

Idaline is still asleep by the time I'm completely ready for work. I leave her be while I walk across the hall to Sawyer's room. I smile when I see him pulling himself up.

"Mornin', son. Any idea on what DaDa should do with you today?" I ask as I pick him up. He babbles eagerly as we work on the diaper change and get him dressed. "Do I take you with me to work? There's more people there. Most importantly, I'm there. Or do I leave you here with Grandma, Nana, and Idaline since if Lila comes around, she'll probably wait until I'm here?"

Sawyer answers, but I'm not sure which way he wants to go. When I stand him up to kiss his forehead and to pick him up, he smiles his little toothy grin and shouts, "Ahda!" He bounces up and down with excitement. I glance over my shoulder to see Idaline.

"Well, someone really likes you," I laugh, placing Sawyer on the floor and watching with pure happiness as he runs over to Idaline.

"Why, though?" she asks with confusion. Idaline bends down to be eye-level with him and he hugs her.

"He knows when he's met a good person." Idaline doesn't seem to accept this answer. "Plus, he likes fresh meat." That makes her laugh. "Come on; let's have breakfast."

The three of us eating breakfast together? It's heaven. The missing piece of my life is here and she fits in seamlessly. But I remember my mother asking about whether or not Idaline would want to be in a relationship when I have a son. Whether she'll eventually be ready to take on that role as his mother, because that's exactly where this will lead. Should I find out if she's prepared to do that before we go any further?

If she says no, would that really separate us? Because I still wouldn't want her to go anywhere. Sawyer will work his magic on her as long as she's here. She'll fall in love with him and change her mind. I just can't see a possibility of Idaline being totally opposed to life with Sawyer and me.

"What are you thinking about over there?" Idaline asks.

"Something my mom said."

Idaline nods at first, but then she says, "Do you want to talk about it?"

I hesitate for a fraction of a second before tossing caution to the wind. This is Idaline. We can talk about anything. "She was worried about if you'd still be up for a relationship with me since Sawyer is involved." Idaline's eyes widen. "I know I caught you off guard with that and you weren't expecting him, but you're ready to be here with both of us, right?"

She's quiet as she glances over at Sawyer who happily eats his breakfast. Her eyes meet mine with a fierce determination. "I'll do anything to be with you. Sawyer is something I wasn't prepared for, but it's not like I'll haul ass back home because of him. He'll be worth staying for just as much as you are."

God, I love her. Just when I think she can't get any better, after all these years of knowing her, she proves me wrong.

Our breakfast ends nicely. I decide to keep Sawyer at home where there's a locked door between him and whoever may be on the other side. My mom and nana are made to come over, even though only one of them is needed. This is partly because Idaline made appointments to look at some apartments. I'm a tad disappointed to hear this, as I would've liked to go with her, but I can't take off at the last minute. Well, Brent may actually let me because he's that nice, but I don't want to find out.

LIGHT IN THE DARK

Whenever I have a free moment at work, I'm texting someone at home to check in on Sawyer. Everything has been quiet. No visits from Lila, which quite frankly just puts me on edge. Lila won't disappear quietly into the night like a good person. And I'm proven right when I'm leaving work and she's sitting on the hood of my car.

A ton of emotions hits me like a brick. Fury, dread, fear, and anxiety are at the top of the list.

"Stalking me now?" I ask when I'm within ten feet of her. I focus on her bruise, hoping it's enough of a distraction because just the sight of her puts tequila on the forefront on my mind and has my mouth salivating for the taste.

"We need to talk."

"No, we don't. Having a restraining order kind of prevents that," I remind her. I pull my phone out to call the cops because I'm not messing around. I don't have to talk to her and I don't want to. Lila jumps off my car, rushes over, and snatches my phone from me. "Lila," I sigh. "Give my phone back."

"I want you back, FC. We were so good together. I even gave Sawyer to you!"

"You're fucking crazy if you think I'd ever get back together with you. Or that we were good together for that matter. Hand over my phone." I hold my hand out, but it's useless. One thing I won't do is try to wrestle it away from her. She's not about to say I put my hands on her in any way.

"I know we needed time apart and that you needed to see I would do anything to be with you, even if it meant giving Sawyer to you, and I did that. I gave up my rights, so you would see I was a good mother and that you would see I'm a good person. My life sucks, FC, and it was better when you were in it."

I laugh, making her frown. "You were a good mother? A good person?" A hysterical laugh bubbles out of me again. "A good mother saw her son when she still had rights. A good person doesn't do this!" I whirl around and lift my shirt so she can see the scars she left. Before I can pull my shirt down, she's touching my back with a gentleness that doesn't match her personality. Swiveling on my heels, I grab her wrist with my phone, peel her fingers off of it, and release her. "Don't you ever fucking touch me again."

As I walk around her to my car, in the calmest of voices, she says, "This isn't over, FC."

It damn sure isn't because unless Lila decides to leave me alone, she'll continue to be a nightmare in my life. Feeling her touch makes me want to go home and shower with a bottle of tequila. Her exploring my scars for all of a second is completely different than when Idaline did so last night. Idaline was concerned and worried. No doubt remembering how I kept my back turned away from her the last time we were naked together, when my back was still healing from what Lila did to me.

She wanted to know exactly what happened and I reluctantly gave her the details of that night while she placed soft kisses all across my back. It felt like it took forever for the tension to leave me. I despise those scars and I'm not looking forward to the day Sawyer asks what happened to me. I may have my son and be glad Lila isn't involved, but that doesn't mean I'm looking forward to one day telling him the truth of why she isn't in his life. If he asks, I'll tell him. I don't plan to lie.

I just hope he waits a long time before asking me about her.

When I get home, my three favorite women, plus my dad, are in the kitchen laughing. So much for not over-whelming Idaline too soon. Although, part of that is my fault. I check over her body language first as I walk closer to make sure she's comfortable. Appears so. She smiles when she spots me and I kiss her cheek.

Sawyer bangs on his highchair table, calling out my name. I walk over to kiss the top of his head and say hello to him.

"How was your day?" Dad asks.

"Fine until Lila showed up." Happiness leaves each of their faces. I recount what happened as I pick Sawyer up, needing to hold him close and reassure myself he's happy and safe, even though I know he's not what Lila wants. She barely mentioned him.

My family tosses out all sorts of ideas on how I need to handle the situation with Lila. My eyes keep straying to Idaline, though, who focuses on her meal and stays quiet. Once conversation dies down, thankfully, I'm able to speak to her.

"How was your day, love?"

Her gaze lifts with surprise. As if she wasn't expect-ing the conversation to turn to her. "I found a place to rent. Looks like I should go home to pack soon."

"Where is the place?" I ask.

"A few miles down the road. Now, I just need to hear about a job."

"We can go this weekend to pack," I tell her, causing Mom to offer to keep Sawyer for me. My heart says he should go with me, while my mind says it may be easier to pack without him walking and crawling around. I still have a few days before I decide on whether or not I'll bring him with me.

"You could bring him," Idaline says, reading the anxiety on my face. "My grandpa could come over and keep an eye on him."

I laugh. "Grandpa McAllister? He doesn't like me, remember?"

Idaline's smile soothes my soul. "He'll like Sawyer, though."

Now that, I don't doubt. Being here, home with my son, Idaline, and my family, I begin to relax. Thoughts about relapsing and drowning myself with a bottle of tequila move to the back of my mind. The volume gets turned way down to a manageable whisper instead of a shout. This is what I need to remind myself of whenever Lila is near. My son, Idaline, and my family are way more important than whatever she's up to or the drink I may want to take. She will not drag me down into the darkness again.

CHAPTER five

Idaline

I n the end, Mrs. Hart convinces FC to leave Sawyer behind. It takes a lot of persuading from his family; I stay out of it. FC goes back and forth on whether to bring him or not. And even as we're leaving, I can see the uncertainty on his face. We drive separately, just in case we need more room for my things, and every time I look into my rearview mirror, I can sense his worry from my own car.

My soul whirls out to seep into his car, as if to comfort him. When we finally arrive at my apartment, it feels so weird, yet familiar to walk in with FC.

"Hey, whatever happened to Mr. Fish?" FC asks as we set our bags down by the door.

"He died a few months ago."

Sadness crosses his features and I fall in love a little more. "I'm sorry, love." He steps forward to hug me. "We can get new fish. Have a tank at my house. Sawyer would love that, I bet."

I lean back to look at him. "That means I have to come to your house to look at the fish."

FC grins. "I know." He kisses me quickly. "Do you want to grab some food, relax for just a bit, and then start some packing before bed?"

"Let's order something."

FC nods in agreement. "You do that then. I'm calling to check on Sawyer." He runs a hand through his hair. "This is the first time I've ever left him for anything other than work. That's stressful enough on its own without me thinking about Lila being nearby."

Oh. That is a big deal. I mean, I knew he was likely anxious over Lila, but he definitely has a reason to be anxious considering this is his first time away from his son. I leave him to make his phone call while I figure out what we should eat and place an order for something to be delivered. FC's voice changes the moment he talks to Sawyer. It softens and turns all sugary sweet. It's freaking adorable to listen to him talk to his son.

And he talks to him or his mother until our food arrives. We sit at my dining table and eat quietly at first. All we have to pack is my personal belongings. This place came furnished and I made sure to find a furnished apartment in Raleigh as well. It's nice to be back at this table with FC, but at the same time, the air feels different.

"Are you happy we're doing this?" FC asks.

I frown with confusion. "Yes, of course." Being with FC is all I've ever wanted; why wouldn't I be happy now that it's finally happening? "Are you?"

He nods. "This is a big change, especially for you. I need to make sure you're okay is all. I need for this to work, Idaline. We need to be open and honest about everything. We need to talk about the hard stuff and work through it. We need to rely on each other. I won't be able to survive losing you if this doesn't work out. You remember what I told you, right?"

I nod, struggling to swallow with the tears welling in my eyes. He's referring to the night he told me I was the one person he can't imagine living without. I reach over to hold his hand. "I promise to do my best and when that isn't good enough, you have permission to reel me back in."

FC smiles and squeezes my hand. "Same for you, love."

"There is one thing that worries me." FC's eyes sear into me. "Not like truly worries me, but worries me in the sense that it's overwhelming to think about right now."

"What is it?" he asks.

"The weight of our future."

FC frowns, looks a bit confused, and sets his fork down. He tugs on my hand. "Come here," he says softly. I stand and move to sit in his lap, straddling him since that's how he positions me. "Explain it to me."

A horrifying thought hits me. "What if you get upset?"

"I won't," he promises.

I'm not sure I believe that, but I trust if he does get upset, we'll work our way through it. So, with a deep breath, I begin to explain myself. "I know a romantic relationship is still new to us, but I feel like our future is already set in stone and I don't know." I glance down at his stomach where I've chosen to rest my hands. "Knowing that we sort of expect to get married one day, knowing that you expect me to help raise Sawyer..." My voice trails off. That's the most overwhelming part.

Knowing that I'm already essentially entering the role of mother, even if it's not official yet. It's what is expected to happen, which means I might as well somewhat start acting the part now. I know I'm twenty-seven, but I still feel like kids are a long ways off if I were to ever have them. And now, with no preparation, there's this beautiful little boy in my life.

What if I mess up? What if he decides he doesn't like me? What if we don't bond? These questions tumble out of my mouth before FC has a chance to speak. "What if I can't handle it? What if I'm not meant to be a mother? What if it turns out I like kids better when I can return them to their parents and not have them around twenty-four seven? We'll be one of those couples who forever lives separately, never gets married, and dates for years and years because it'll turn out I don't want kids of my own."

FC clamps a hand over my mouth. "Calm down, Idaline. Your anxiety is talking and I need you to come back to me. I'll remove my hand, but I want you to stay quiet and listen to me carefully." When I nod in agreement, he removes his hand. "All these questions are nothing but your anxiety getting the best of you." I frown and shake my head in disagreement. "Yes, it is, love. Sawyer already likes you. We'll both mess up. We're not perfect.

"You've already started to bond. You can handle it because we'll be doing it together. And you do want kids one day. You wouldn't have that list of favorite names if you didn't want to be a mother. I'm sorry you're feeling pressured; that's the last thing I wanted for you. You take things at your pace, okay? But instead of being over-whelmed that our future seems to be set in stone, maybe you can find comfort in knowing where we'll end up."

He does have a point. I lean forward to rest my fore-head against his. "Maybe it was my anxiety talking."

FC smiles. "It was. Some are legitimate concerns, but you were getting carried away, too."

Feeling a bit better about things, I return to my own seat to finish eating. We tidy up and then decide to start with my bedroom. That's where the bulk of my things are. Might as well get the biggest mess out of the way, right? It won't be prettily packed either because we only have two vehicles to pack with as much shit as possible.

"Do you think you'll be happy in Raleigh?" FC asks after we've steadily worked for about twenty minutes.

"Yeah, I think so," I answer honestly. "Aside from you, it seems like a nice place. If I can get a job, things would be complete."

He nods in understanding. A few times, he stops to text his mom. Smiling shyly as he admits he's getting an update on his son, which often includes a picture he shows me. We talk more in depth about the past two years of our lives. Him and his relationship with Lila, the birth of his son, and what it's been like as a single parent moving back home close to his parents. I tell him about awkward run-ins with Justin, my issues with anxiety, even where it con-cerns him, and about the time period where we hardly talked at all, especially once I learned his name.

It's cathartic to feel so free with him, freer than ever to communicate and talk about things I might have hesitated with in the past. I think it's likely because he's shared every possible thing about himself that he could. He's opened himself up. He's made himself vulnerable. If FC, who I know is so strong, can make himself vulnerable to tell me about the weakest parts of himself, then so can I.

After two hours of packing, we decide that's good enough for one night. It's quiet as we get ready for bed. FC is first in bed. He lies on his side, one arm stretched out just beneath my pillow. A small smile rests on his face.

"What are you waiting for?" he asks as I stand next to the bed, gazing at him.

"Does it amaze you that we now get to sleep in the same bed? And not as friends, but as lovers?" I wiggle my eyebrows, which makes him laugh.

He reaches over, grabs my wrist, and tugs me hard. "Do you know what amazes me?" he asks once I'm lying comfortably next to him.

"What?" I whisper.

"That you could love me. That you still love me. That you're willing to be with me. Everything about you amazes me."

I grin. One kiss leads to two and two kisses lead to our hands exploring each other's bodies, which eventually leads to heavy breathing, moans, and the best sex ever.

We spend all day Saturday packing and finish in time to drive over to my grandpa's house to eat dinner with my family. Considering this huge change I'm making, they all want to see me before I leave and they would like to meet FC. I think we're both a bit nervous. Neither of us really have a reason to be, but we are all the same.

We enter my grandpa's house holding hands, feeling like a team ready to face a firing squad if need be. My parents and my grandpa sit in the living room. They laugh over something we obviously missed since we weren't inside when they were talking.

"Hey, y'all," I say to announce our arrival.

Heads turn, smiles stay in place, and they stand. Grandpa is closest, so he's the first to pull me into a bear hug.

"I sure have missed you. Going to miss you even more now that you're moving away." He releases me, but rests his hands on my shoulders. "But you can still call me if you need me and I'll get in the old pick-up and be on my way."

My smile is a little wobbly because he's made me all emotional now. "Thanks, Grandpa. You remember FC, right?"

"I do," he nods curtly, reaching out to shake his hand. "It's good to see you. I sure hope you plan to take good care of my granddaughter."

"I do," FC replies seriously.

I turn to my parents. "Mom, Dad, this is FC Hart. FC, meet my mom, Heidi, and my dad, Simon."

The hellos are exchanged easily before Grandpa leads us all to his dining room table where food is already laid out. We take seats and begin to distribute food while questions are fired at us both. Silently, I thank my grandfather because my parents never ask me if I'm sure I should be moving to North Carolina. Instead, I get questions like have I found an apartment and a job. Or how often I plan to come back home for visits.

When they learn of FC's son, it's as if they learn they just became grandparents themselves and they definitely want us to either return with him soon or visit us as soon as they can. FC shows off pictures of Sawyer like the proud father he is. Speaking of Sawyer also gives him the excuse to call and check in, which allows my parents to see Sawyer and talk to him since it's a video call. They fall in love immediately with Sawyer.

For the most part, FC freely shares the fact that he has sole custody of Sawyer and why. He doesn't give them any gritty details, but he surprises me when he tells them it's because Lila abused him and honestly didn't care about Sawyer. The more FC talks, the more my parents seem to like him and the more my grandpa seems to re-spect him. I honestly couldn't have imagined a better din-ner, especially once things become more of a relaxed con-versation instead of a targeted question and answer ses-sion.

Before the night is over with, FC promises that they can meet Sawyer.

Everything is all packed at my apartment, but he sur-prises me when he doesn't want to take advantage of the additional night we can stay.

"I really hate to ask this, Idaline, but do you mind if we head home tonight? I'm having Sawyer withdrawals."

"If that's what you want to do, I'm okay with it."

His gorgeous smile blooms on his face and he leans over the console to kiss me. "Thank you. I know we should probably stay and have one more night with just the two of us, but I can't take it anymore."

"Then let's head home."

We first drop by my apartment, so I can leave my keys and pick up my car. FC called ahead, so his mom is at his apartment with Sawyer. When we get there, he bypasses his mother and walks straight to Sawyer's bedroom. His mother chuckles.

"I'm surprised he lasted this long to be honest," she tells me.

I smile. "Me too."

"If you need any help unpacking, let me know, okay?"

"Thanks."

"I'm going to head on home; it's late. Tell FC I'll talk to him tomorrow." His mother gives me a hug and then she's out the door.

I walk down the hallway and find FC in Sawyer's room. He stands over the crib, silently watching his son. I walk to his side and look down at him as well. FC takes my hand in his.

"I can't explain how relieved I feel to come home and find him safe and sound, exactly as I left him. But I keep expecting to see something different. Like did he grow at all while I was gone? Did he eat something new? Do something new? Did he miss me like I missed him? Did he wonder why I was gone? Did he think I left him? Was he scared?" FC glances at me. "I kinda want to wake him up and give him a big hug. Let him know I'm home."

Whether he should or not, I don't know. I'm not a parent. So I give the only advice that I can. "He's your kid; do what you want or what you think you should do."

FC rests his gaze on Sawyer for all of five seconds before he mutters, "Fuck it," and picks his son up. Sawyer whines for a second due to being woken up, but FC quickly soothes him. "Don't worry, son. I'll let you go right back to sleep in a second." Hearing FC's voice wakes Sawyer up even more. He lifts his head from FC's shoulder and stares at his father.

"Hey," FC whispers. "I missed you. Can I have some sugar?" Sawyer plants a slobbery kiss on FC and then reveals a toothy smile. "That's my boy. Come on; let's lay down."

We move over into FC's room. He lays Sawyer in the middle of the bed and then we change and get ready for bed ourselves. FC climbs into bed and Sawyer crawls onto his chest. I lie squarely on my side, watching them with a smile on my face. FC rubs Sawyer's back, lulling him back to sleep, and then looks over at me.

He slides his arm out. "Scoot over here. I need my favorite people with me."

Well, he doesn't need to tell me twice. Sawyer turns his head at the movement of me coming closer. His sleepy eyes watch me warily.

"Hey, Sawyer," I whisper.

My heart warms when he reaches out and rests his tiny little hand on my face. "Ahda."

"Yep. That's me."

"The kid is breaking my heart in the best way possible," FC says with a happy sigh.

LIGHT IN THE DARK

Sawyer pulls his hand back and snuggles in closer to FC. We stay quiet, soon falling asleep.

CHAPTER Six

FC

We're utterly exhausted after unloading all of Idaline's things from our vehicles. Idaline swears she'll unpack herself later. I'll worry about actually helping her at another time. Sawyer was a champ today while we worked and I think we all deserve a celebration.

I stand with Sawyer on my hip and hold my hand out to Idaline. "May we take you out? You don't mind if our first date includes Sawyer and happens after a hard day's work, do you?"

Idaline smiles. She takes my hand and stands. "I would love to go on a date with you both."

We gather Sawyer's diaper bag, decide on where to go, and drive to the restaurant. The restaurant gets a failing grade right from the start because Sawyer needs a diaper change; there isn't a changing table or anywhere I can change his diaper in the men's bathroom. I'm two seconds away from simply walking into the women's bathroom because surely they have one, but I decide maybe I should ask Idaline if she'll do it for me.

"Back already?" Idaline asks with surprise when I return to the table.

"There's not a changing table in the men's room. Do you mind taking him into the women's bathroom and changing him for me?"

Her eyes widen to the size of saucers. "I've never..." Her voice trails off as she shakes her head.

"It's not hard and he behaves."

She swallows hard, but stands. The moment she holds her hands out, Sawyer reaches for her too and goes to her. I slip the diaper bag onto her shoulder. Her eyes are full of worry, but I know she's got this. It's so easy. We walk to the bathroom together, as I plan to stand outside, just in case she needs me.

Idaline slips into the bathroom. It seems like she's only in there for a minute before I hear, "FC! Oh god!" I rush into the bathroom. "Everything okay?" I ask as I hear her gag.

"No. He shit." She gags again and I can't help it. I bust out laughing as I walk over to the changing table. Idaline glares at me. "I thought it would just be a wet diaper. I'm not prepared for this." She walks as far away as she can with her hand over her nose. "Why haven't you potty trained him yet?"

"He's only one," I remind her as I quickly change his diaper and then wash my hands. "I didn't realize a little shit would make you react like that," I say with a little laugh.

Idaline glares at me. "How did that even come out of him? Is it always like that?"

I shrug, not wanting to turn her off completely from diaper changes.

Idaline gets a little more involved in other ways, though. Back at the table, while we talk, we take turns feeding Sawyer. This is a more enjoyable task for her. My heart doesn't know what to do watching the two of them.

"I love you." Idaline glances up at me. "And I'm extremely lucky that you've decided to move here. That you're with me." I shake my head in wonder. "I don't know why you are, but I'm glad nonetheless."

Idaline frowns. "You don't know why?"

It's not until she asks that I even realize what I said. That I meant it. That I have invisible scars in addition to my physical ones from Lila. That her voice is in the back of my mind, reminding me what a worthless, no-good man I am. Did she affect me more than I thought? Why in the fuck would I worry about being with Idaline when I never have before?

"FC?" Idaline questions softly.

I shake my head to bring myself back to the present. "You're with me because I'm so damn handsome." For good measure, I smile and throw in a wink.

Thankfully, Sawyer steals our attention with some of his talk and his smile. It's hard to believe we're here on a date, even with Sawyer. There were many times when I thought this would never happen, yet it is. My heart wants to burst with happiness. It almost seems too good to be true.

LIGHT IN THE DARK

"What else do you need to do to settle in?" I ask, causing her to sigh a little.

"Aside from finding a job and unpacking, I need to find a new therapist and psychiatrist." Idaline frowns and almost looks as if she'll be sick. "I don't like the idea of this at all. I'm hoping I can convince Mrs. Judith to let me do video sessions with her instead of finding someone new. A psychiatrist, I'm okay with, but not her."

"What if she can't? Does she have any contacts up here to recommend?"

Idaline shrugs.

"I could always be your therapist," I say in a completely serious voice, even though I'm teasing.

She laughs and crouches a little to be eye-level with Sawyer. "Your daddy is crazy, but he makes us laugh, so it's okay."

Our food arrives and Sawyer would climb out of his highchair if he wasn't strapped in. My boy is hungry and everyone in the restaurant knows as he slaps the table and shouts, "Nom! Nom! Nom!" We can't help but laugh, especially since I essentially taught him this behavior. Idaline surprises me when she takes a little spoonful of her mashed potatoes and feeds it to him. Sawyer sits back and hums in appreciation.

Idaline may be concerned about how we'll sew our three lives together, but she has nothing to worry about. She effortlessly weaves her way in and probably doesn't even realize it herself. She may think nothing of feeding Sawyer some food, but she should. It's not something she has to do. But she did and she did it without asking. To me, that shows some level of comfort. It also shows how much she already cares about Sawyer to take the initiative.

"What do you see for your future?" she asks. "You stopped answering me before and now I know why. You can answer me this time."

I want to answer, but I also worry that maybe I might scare her. At the same time, I want to lay it all on the line. To let her know how much I love her and how important she is to me and my future. If she knows exactly how involved I want her in my future, then that'll at least give her a glimpse at how willing I am to fight for that future with her.

With a deep breath, I level a stare at her and say, "My future looks like me working at the shop with the Murphys, you working wherever makes you happy, us eventually living in the same home with Sawyer. You being a mother figure to him." Idaline sheds a few tears at hearing me say so. "Maybe, if it's okay with you, he'll eventually call you mom and you can adopt him as your own if you wish. One day, we'll buy a house because we'll need more room for another baby. One day, you'll walk down the aisle during the wedding of your dreams and we'll recite vows. And at some point, far off in the future, we'll be old and wrinkly, sitting on our front porch in a pair of rocking chairs, talking about all of the people that go by the house. That's my future."

Idaline wipes away some tears, but I notice her chest moving faster than it was before. "I love you." Her eyes shut tightly. A steady stream of air leaves her mouth.

"You okay, love?" I ask as I feed a small bite of food to Sawyer.

"I'm calming my nerves. It's still overwhelming to think about all of that." She opens her eyes. "But I promise I want a future with you too."

I smile and let the subject drop. Idaline knows how best to calm her nerves and I don't want to make things worse for her. We eat in silence before she abruptly stands, pulls me out of my side of the booth, and slides in. I reclaim my seat as she pulls her plate across the table. Idaline leans against my shoulder while she continues to eat.

"Ahda! Nom." Idaline lifts her head as Sawyer holds out the piece of food I just gave him.

"Oh, you're special," I say. "He never shares his food."

Idaline smiles, pushes his hand toward his mouth, and says, "You eat it."

Sawyer frowns. "Ahda!" he shouts. He jabbers away, sound angry that she refused.

"I think you better eat it," I say.

She takes the tiny piece of food from Sawyer and eats it while humming as if it's the best thing she's ever tasted. Sawyer's eyes light up. And that begins a new game of sorts for Sawyer where he and Idaline take turns sharing their food. As dinner winds down, Sawyer gets cranky, ready for bed. He throws down a piece of food and reaches for me with a whine. I remove him from his seat and he snuggles against my chest with his head on my shoulder. The faster we can pay our bill and get out of here, the better.

We make it home, but not before Sawyer falls asleep and not before we're confronted by Lila once more. She sits outside my apartment door. The moment I spot her, I pull Idaline behind me and call the cops to report her. Unfortunately, Lila spots us before I can quietly back up out of view.

"FC, wait!" She hurries to stand and rushes toward us.

"The police are on their way," I warn her. "I don't know how many times I have to tell you I don't want you and that you can't break the restraining order."

Her eyes narrow as she stops three feet away. "Did you take your babysitter out with you?"

I don't answer that. It's none of her business.

She takes a step closer and reaches out as if she may touch my sleeping son. I twist until my back faces her, so Sawyer is closest to Idaline, and snarl, "Don't you fucking dare touch him."

"He's my son, too."

"Not since you gave up your rights."

A siren can just barely be heard and that's all it takes for Lila's features to smooth. "Tell your slut she might as well move back to South Carolina because we're getting back together, FC." She brushes past us to hurry to the elevator.

She's gone by the time the cops show up. I don't know if we should've tried to keep her here, or if that would've looked bad for me since she was trying to leave. Then again, the only reason she wanted to leave was because the cops were coming. Next time, she won't get a warning.

I don't like the fact that Lila pointed out that she recognized Idaline. I don't like that she's here again. That she thinks she has any claim to Sawyer. It's so difficult putting Sawyer in his bed for the night rather than holding him in my arms. It's difficult especially considering I'm more on edge than before, which means I want to drink or smoke. Both of those aren't an option for me. Sawyer will never smell the stench of tobacco or nicotine on me, nor will he have an alcoholic for a father.

"Will you stay here with him?" I ask Idaline, who stands in the doorway of his room.

"Where are you going?"

"I need to burn the tension away, so I'm going over to the gym. It's on the complex, so you can call if you need me and I can be right back within minutes." I lift my gaze from Sawyer to Idaline. "I need to do something other than sit here."

"Okay. Do what you need to do. We'll be here when you get back."

I walk over and kiss her before heading to my room to change. There's almost a touch of resistance wrapped around my limbs. I guess part of me thinks I should stay, lean on Idaline, and be close to Sawyer. But the edginess eats away at my soul and I need to soothe it away. The quickest way to do this is by exercising.

Idaline moved to stand by my door while I was changing and she blocks my exit now that I'm done. Her eyes crinkle in worry. Her lips dip slightly in a frown.

"Will you be okay?" she asks.

"Yes." If I'm not when I get back, I'll make sure I am by the morning.

She steps out of the way and off I go. The gym is only two buildings over from mine in the main building where the management office is located. There are various things I do when I come here. The treadmill allows me to run until my legs feel as if they're on the verge of cramping and losing all feeling until I collapse. The benchpress builds muscles in my arms and allows me to keep keep lifting the weights until I worry the bar will get stuck on top of my chest. There are other machines I use and use until I feel like my muscles will give out.

When I work out, I focus only on the task at hand and nothing else. I don't try to work through my thoughts or whatever may be worrying me. The entire point is to get away from that, to loosen the tension flowing through my veins, to be too tired afterward to think about my life. I'm not sure how long I spend at the gym, but I'm nearly too tired to walk back to my apartment by the time I decide I should head back.

Halfway to my apartment, I hear a soft whispered, "FC!"

No.

No, no, no. I just spent at least an hour in the gym because of this woman. Why is she here again?

Slowly, I turn around. There, a few feet away, Lila stands with a slightly worried look on her face.

"Please give me ten minutes, FC." What sucks is that I see the Lila I first met. The sweet girl who seemed to want nothing more than to be loved and taken care of, but apparently has a serious dark and evil side hidden beneath the surface. What sucks even more is that I see that side of her and I *still* feel like I owe something to her. Like she deserves to be heard, that she deserves my time, because maybe, just maybe, there's a tiny heart inside that chest of hers. I know better than that, yet I still find myself nodding my head.

"Say whatever you want. You have five minutes."

The relief is evident as her shoulders relax and she gives me a small smile. Lila comes closer, but she's smart enough to stay two feet away from me. And I listen as she gives me her side of the story.

"Mom told me that you'd be more willing to get back together with me if I gave up my rights because it meant I would be looking out for Sawyer's best interest and giving you what you want. I figured I would do that, wait a few months, and then reach out to you. But you moved away and," she glances down as if in shame, "I met someone."

Lila looks up at me for a reaction, but my expression is emotionless. She sighs a little, but continues. "Things were great for a while. Then everything changed and he became abusive. I didn't know how to get away. I thought about calling you." At this, I snort because I'm honestly not sure I would've helped her. Lila frowns. "Our relationship was pretty toxic, but I was finally able to end it and now, here I am. I want to be with you, FC. I love you. You should be with me, not that South Carolina slut. I messed up and I'm sorry, but things will be different this time around. So, what do you say?" She looks so hopeful, but I have no issues with what I'm about to say.

"No. Hell no. Please go back home." I turn to leave and that's when Lila's true colors burst free. She takes a swing at me as rage explodes on her face, contorting her features into something ugly. She misses my face and hits my shoulder. It's in that split second that I realize I forgot my phone. Lila begins to scream, but I keep walking.

"You can't do this to me! We belong together! I won't stand for this! It's because of that girl, isn't?"

And it goes on and on until I finally reach my apartment. I worked so hard to get rid of the stress she gave me only for her to show back up and give it all back to me again. The temptation to slip into the darkness by finding something to drink looms over me, but that can't be an option. I need to figure out how to get rid of Lila.

CHAPTER Seven

Idaline

Yelling from outside sends my heartbeat galloping faster and faster. I hurry to the door, but before I can peer through the peephole, FC storms through the door, slams it shut behind him, and locks it. He sees me and relaxes.

"Come here, love," he says softly as Lila shouts something about getting revenge. I hurry to him and he wraps me in his arms as tight as he can. "It won't be easy to get away from her, but as long as I have you and Sawyer to keep me grounded, we'll be okay." He kisses my forehead. "Let me take my shower and then we'll go to bed."

Things suddenly quieten outside as he leads me toward his bedroom. Before I know what I'm doing, I blurt out, "Shouldn't I go home?"

FC nearly breaks his neck when he looks back at me. "No. I don't want to risk you running into her and it's late.

You should stay here tonight." He tugs me down the hall-way. "You should take a shower with me. Let's wash the filth of her memory away."

There's no sense in arguing with him. I allow him to lead me to the bathroom. My breathing is unsteady as we slowly undress each other, steam building in the bathroom. If I didn't know FC loved me, if he hadn't said the words, I know by the way he looks at me. I can feel it with his touch. And when he kisses me, his love consumes my very soul, reminding it to whom it belongs and of our bright future together.

There's nothing special about our shower other than we're both here together and FC eyes me with such a heat-ed gaze. After we dry off, FC grabs my wrists before I can grab my pajamas.

"We don't need those right now," he says with a smirk.

"What do we need?" I ask.

He walks us backward until my legs bump into the bed. "We need some lovin' from each other. Don't you agree?" His hands slide up my back while his head dips to drop kisses on my neck and shoulder. My body lights with the fire he sets with his every touch. He somehow sends my heartbeat accelerating while steadying it all the same.

Sex with FC makes the world complete just as much as when he looks at me or holds my hands or tells me he loves me or says something sweet. It brings us so much closer each and every time. I have never felt as cherished and loved as I do when I'm with FC. How one person can emit so many emotions? It's overwhelmingly perfect.

"What are you thinking?" FC asks me afterward.

"I think you make me too happy for words."

FC smiles. "Right back at you, love. Let's get some sleep." He kisses my forehead and pulls me in tight.

Snuggling with him and falling asleep in his arms is heaven on earth.

In the morning, Nana comes over, FC leaves for work, and I leave for my apartment. FC doesn't like the idea of me unpacking alone, but I'm looking forward to the time to do so. I'm hoping beyond all hopes that I hear about a job soon. My anxiety is low, but constant, and the longer I wait, the worse it'll get.

With some music playing from my phone, I begin to unpack my things. It's blissful, actually. Doing all of these things means I'm not thinking about Lila, needing a job, my new relationship and responsibilities. My mind is a carefree blank. Well, mostly. It's been on my mind what FC said. How maybe we should get some fish.

If I can get everything unpacked, then maybe Nana and Sawyer would like to go with me to pick everything out. Then again, that might be something FC would want to do with us. How long does it take to hear about a job anyway? Can't I hear about one today? That would be pretty awesome. I probably shouldn't buy fish until I find a job. I need to be smart about my money before I run out of it.

Miraculously, I finish unpacking. After a call to my grandpa to check in with him, I lay on the bed to revel in my accomplishments. I'm freaking exhausted. Add on to a steady stream of anxiety because my mind thinks I should've heard about a job already and I'm even more tired.

"Idaline?" a quiet masculine voice says.

I stir from a sleep I apparently fell into, open my eyes, and see FC and Sawyer sitting on the edge of my bed. I gave FC the spare key to my house; otherwise, I would be concerned with how he got into my apartment.

"What are you doing here?" I ask as I sit up.

"You weren't answering your cell and I was worried. You got so much done today. No wonder you wanted a nap."

"I actually didn't mean to fall asleep."

"Ahda." Sawyer crawls over to me with his toy in hand and shows it off to me.

I entertain him, happy to see them both. With a quick glance at a nearby clock, I see it's way past dinner time.

"Hungry?" FC asks.

"Nom!" Sawyer shouts, causing us to laugh.

"Looks like two of us are hungry," I say.

"He's always hungry if food is brought up. I may have already ordered something since I know you haven't been grocery shopping yet. It should be here soon."

FC is the best. We move into the living room, where we play, have dinner, and then I say goodbye to FC and Sawyer. Living in a new place is always weird and it always gives me some anxieties. At least I can do my best to shrug it off as normal nerves. FC checks in every now and then before we go to bed, and that helps soothe me.

But my anxiety goes insane the next day. There's not much for me to do, other than complete some grocery shopping and wait around, hoping I hear about a job. If I'm not walking around the apartment, I'm sitting with my knees bouncing, my fingers constantly tingling, and my heart beating too fast. I also get referred to a new therapist, who I'm supposed to see tomorrow. I'd much rather be interviewed for a job.

What if I never get a job? Then what? What if my previous employer gives a bad reference because of how I left? How will I survive then? Maybe I should calculate how many days my money will last me.

A day goes by and on the second, I feel even worse. I need to hear something from someone. There's a knock on my door around noon. Thinking it's FC, I open the door without checking the peephole first. When I see Lila, my heart stops. My body freezes. I don't even have the chance to slam the door closed.

Lila pushes her way past me. "Thanks for letting me in. Idaline, right? Took me a long time to remember that."

I turn and face her, closing the door. "What do you want?"

She laughs. "I want you to leave FC."

"So you can abuse him again?"

Her mouth drops in outrage and shock. "I never did such a thing! Is that what you think? I mean, look at me and look at FC. How in the world would I abuse him? Every couple has arguments, Idaline. That's all that happened between FC and me. And now, here you are, ruining what we're supposed to have together. Do you get off being a homewrecker?"

I stare at her for a moment. Is she serious? Does she truly believe the words coming out of her mouth? "You're delusional," I say the very words I'm thinking. "FC doesn't have scars on his back from an accident or simple arguments. Those are from *you* and your hatefulness. He didn't have black eyes and bruises from anyone other than *you*. I don't know what you're doing here, and quite frankly, I don't care. But you aren't welcome and you'll never have FC. Not because of me, but because of you and what you did to him."

I've never seen eyes light up with an evil glow before now. The slap comes before I have a chance to blink. My cheek burns. Did she seriously just hit me? There's another knock on my door and I rush to answer it.

FC. Thankfully.

He sees me and my reddening cheek. He glances behind me and sees Lila. And that same fury I saw before in Lila's eyes fills FC's. He storms past me, grabs her arm, and drags her out of the apartment, nearly throwing her out of it.

"Stay the *fuck* away from her. My patience is gone, Lila. *Gone*. Go home and don't ever come back." He slams the door, locks it, and then turns to face me. "Why in the hell would you let her in here?"

"I didn't!" I shout, angry that he's directing his anger at me. "I opened the door, thinking it was you, and she barged in. She slapped me, FC! I could blame you for that because she's *your* ex-girlfriend. What are you doing?" I snap as he steps forward and wraps his arms around me.

"I'm sorry," he whispers. "I was angry at her and worried for you. Let's breathe and calm down."

"I don't want to calm down," I pout. "I'm mad you yelled at me."

FC chuckles. "Then be mad at me while I take you out to lunch. And let me give you a kiss."

I pretend to think about it before pursing my lips and allowing FC to get himself a kiss. "I'm not up for lunch," I confess. "My anxiety has been insane the last two days."

He frowns, not at all happy to hear about this. "Then you should leave. You've been cooped up here too long. Some fresh air and a new scenery might do you some good."

"It doesn't work that way," I say, trying my best not to snap at him and be angry.

He nods. "I know. You've explained it to me enough that I know better, but I don't think hiding in here is helpful either. Let's go and I promise to make it as good as I can for you."

With a sigh, I agree to go. We're both on the paranoid side, looking around for any signs of Lila. We don't see her, so maybe she finally went away. FC calls in to a diner, places an order, and it's ready by the time we get there. He runs inside to grab it and then carts me off to a nearby park. It's too cold and windy to sit outside, but it's nice to see trees and grass, even if it is winter.

"Maybe you should come over tonight," FC suggests. "We could go look for fish if you want."

"That sounds nice."

FC grins, happy that I'm agreeing to get out of the house, but I'm about to ruin it.

"But I should probably sleep at my apartment."

My phone rings with a number I don't recognize. For a moment, I hesitate about answering it, but decide I better. My heart pounds as I listen to the man on the other end. He's from one of the places I applied to and would like to schedule an interview with me tomorrow. It's as if my prayers have been answered. But I'm terrified as well. There's so much pressure on me now.

"Idaline? You got a job interview?"

"Yeah, tomorrow." I look over at him, completely scared to death. "What if I don't get it?"

"Aw, love." He tugs me toward him the best he can with a console between us. "Let's worry about that after the interview and once they've told you you aren't hired. I'm sure you'll do great tomorrow."

I'm sure hoping. FC takes me back home so he can head back to work and I spend the rest of my day worrying about my job interview for tomorrow. FC does come over after work to pick me up. Sawyer looks like a happy little baby and shouts my name as I get into the car.

"Hey, Sawyer," I say to him with a smile. He grins at me. "Do you want to get some fish?"

He answers back, but I'm not sure if he says yes or no. FC gave him a fish stuffed animal to play with, so it seems as if he is ready.

"I figured we would get the tank today, check out the fish, and come back tomorrow once the tank is ready," FC tells me.

That sounds good to me. Sawyer talks in the backseat until we arrive at the store. FC holds Sawyer's hand, letting him walk into the store. It kind of amazes me. He has the patience to walk a little slower, stop when Sawyer finds something of interest, and talk to him about whatever he sees. He's totally entranced by the birds we come by. FC picks him up, so he can see a rabbit that's up for adoption.

And when we get to the fish, Sawyer is in love. He tries to press his face to the glass, but FC doesn't let him get quite that close. Sawyer points to practically all fish.

"We have to find a place for them to live first," FC tells him as we walk toward the tanks and away from the fish. Sawyer twists in FC's arms to look at the retreating fish.

"DaDa!"

FC rubs his back. "We'll get some later. It's okay."

Showing fish to Sawyer first turns out to be a bad idea. All he wants is fish. It's tempting to show him something else, but the last thing I think we should do is show him other animals that he may fall in love with. FC doesn't seem bothered by Sawyer's whines and pleas to see the fish. He soothes him with such gentleness and patience that halfway through picking items out, Sawyer has stopped crying and is making his fish swim like the ones he saw.

"What about this?" FC holds up a decorative item for the tank. "Why are you looking at me like that?"

"I see people be parents all the time, but for some reason when you do it, it just…" I shake my head as my voice trails off. "It amazes me when I watch you. It's almost as if I've never seen someone be a good parent and you're my first example. I love watching you with him." I shrug and focus on the pirate ship in his hand. "I like it."

FC smiles, leans forward, and kisses me chastely and quickly. "I love you."

"I love you too."

Sawyer joins in on the fun and smacks a kiss to FC's cheek.

"I love you too, son."

Gah, they are too adorable. I'm glad FC dragged me out of the house. Or at least, that I'm spending time with them. I'm not anxiety-free, but I don't feel like I'm drowning in it either. My mind is mostly distracted for a bit. The noise, the worry, has quieted to a soft thrum instead of loud, raucous buzzing.

"Do you want to come over and set it up with us?" FC asks as we're checking out.

"I should probably go home. I have a therapy appointment and my interview tomorrow," I remind him, though I would love to go with him. But how am I supposed to get used to my new apartment if I'm spending the nights at his house? And...and...I'm sure there are more reasons why I shouldn't go. Why I feel this way, who knows.

"I'll worry about you if you don't come."

"I can take care of myself."

He sighs as he pushes the cart toward the exit, while I now hold Sawyer. "I know you can take care of yourself." But things are awfully quiet as he drives me to my apartment. He finds a free parking space as close as he can and then turns toward me in his seat. "Just remember that we don't live in two different states anymore. We're only five minutes away from each other. If you need me, you call me or come over."

"I know. No more hiding or running away, I promise."

His smile is relaxed and happy. "I'd walk you to the door, but..." He tilts his head toward the backseat where Sawyer has nodded off.

"I'll be fine."

"Text me when you're safe inside."

That I can do. After a breathtaking kiss, I head inside.

"I've read over the notes from Mrs. Judith, but I would like to hear from you," Mr. Tucker says. "Tell me a little about yourself, your anxieties, and what brings you to Raleigh."

All I can do is stare at him for a moment. My heart is boomeranging around my chest, trying to find a way out. I didn't really know who I was seeing today, and I didn't realize I would be as caught off guard as I am right now. Before I can think about it, I blurt out what's sort of troubling me. "You're a man."

Mr. Tucker, a man at least fifty years old, chuckles. "Yes, ma'am, I am."

"I'm sorry. I'm just used to seeing women. It's happened that way with all my doctors and you're throwing me off here." He's actually giving me anxiety. Will it be different for some reason? Will he be less sympathetic? Is he as good at his job as Mrs. Judith? Why am I even thinking these things?

"Don't worry about it, Idaline. If it makes you feel any better, I know Judith personally and that's how you ended up here. She trusts me to take good care of you and that's what I plan to do."

"You know her?"

Mr. Tucker nods and even smiles. "She's my sister-in-law."

And just like that, a whoosh of relief leaves me. I think back to what he asked of me and begin to talk. By the end of my first session, I decide I like him. Knowing that he knows Mrs. Judith and she trusts him eliminates so many of my anxieties about seeing a new therapist. He has such an easygoing style when he talks and he seems so understanding. He wishes me luck with my job interview, but he'll get an update next week. With everything going on and to partly get me more comfortable with him, and maybe at my request, he's seeing me on a weekly basis for a while.

Now, if I can only tackle my job interview in an hour.

CHAPTER
Eight

FC

When I get home, I'm happy to walk into my apartment and see Idaline. Her mood is kind of off, though. Her smile is half-hearted as she sits on the floor, playing with Sawyer.

"Where's my dad?" I ask as I sit on the floor with them.

"I told him he could head on home."

My eyes widen with surprise. She chose to spend time with Sawyer alone. She felt confident enough to do so. Then I ask, "Is everything okay?"

She shrugs while Sawyer crawls into my lap. He's always happy to see me. "How was your day?" she asks.

"Good. How was yours? Do you think you'll like your new therapist? How did the job interview go?" I'm worried about both considering she doesn't seem that happy.

"Good," she answers quietly. She focuses on Sawyer's fish. "I think I'll like my new therapist and the interview went well. I should hear something by the end of the week."

"What's bothering you then?"

Idaline looks up at me with apprehension. "Lila confronted me again today. She left when I threatened to call the cops. I'm sorry."

"Why are you sorry?" There's nothing that she could possibly have to apologize for. With Sawyer now out of my lap, I crawl over to her and wrap an arm around her shoulders.

"You had a good day and I had to ruin it by telling you about what happened."

Except she hasn't really told me anything. Regardless, I tell her the only thing I possibly can. "You haven't ruined anything. If anyone has, it's Lila. Tell me what happened."

"She was waiting for me when I got home. She ranted about how I was ruining her plan to get back together with you and how I needed to leave you. I'm pretty sure she was drunk. When I threatened to call the police, she stalked off. Lila was really angry."

Boiling rage bubbles up inside of me. Why must she come and interrupt our lives? Before I can let my thoughts loose, Idaline runs her hand up and down my arm.

"Why don't we go out to eat and then get the fish? Let's have a good night together. I brought a bag to sleep over, if that's okay with you?"

It'll make me feel better if she stays here. She's vulnerable when she's over there alone. And I miss her.

LIGHT IN THE DARK

Sawyer bangs a toy against the floor. Here I've been thinking the past couple of months about putting him in daycare. Not now. Not until Lila is out of the picture. I don't want to risk his safety. Sawyer crawls over to me with a big smile. I brush some of his hair off to the side. Pretty soon we'll have to get his hair cut for the first time.

"FC?"

I glance back up at Idaline. "That sounds great. Don't worry about Lila, okay?" Tomorrow, I'll call Karen, Lila's mom, and see if she can't talk some sense into her daughter. Make her go home. "Keep an eye on him for me for a second." Idaline nods. While she does that, I get Sawyer's things together in order for us to leave.

We need to go out and do things to get our minds off the disaster waiting to happen where Lila is concerned. Focus on the happy things in life and not things like drinking, anxiety, anger, and other not so good things. Honestly, one of the great things about having Sawyer is that he can make me smile so easily. He's a tiny little mood booster. Having a bad day? Spend five minutes with him and he'll turn your entire day around.

Idaline and I spend the rest of our evening out with our entire focus on Sawyer. It's as if we both need the distraction from our worries and we're choosing to give Sawyer all of our attention and love. He's enjoying every second of it. When we get to the pet store, Sawyer is tickled to see all of the fish again. We just get a few guppies.

Sawyer is mesmerized when we get home and eventually release the fish into the tank. We set it up next to the couch and he sits as close as he can, staring until he gets bored. Idaline helps me put him to bed, reading to him after his bath.

Idaline curls up on the couch with me afterward. She manages to stay quiet for all of five minutes, which is a feat in and of itself. "FC," she begins softly, "Lila scares me. I don't like that she seems to have focused on me for the time being. And my grandpa and parents were wondering if we wouldn't mind driving back this weekend, so they can meet Sawyer." She takes a deep breath as if saying that stole what she had.

Her fear is understandable in my opinion. "If you want, you can hang here until you get a job and I can essentially escort you home after work or whenever you're ready to go home. That way you're rarely alone and she has less of an opportunity to come up to you. And yes, we can do that. And try not to worry. I'm going to do my best to get her to leave so neither one of us have to deal with her."

"Tell me a secret," she requests, obviously not wanting to stay on this conversation train.

"I wish we could go off on a vacation together. Just the two of us, although I doubt I could leave Sawyer for that long without bugging the hell out of my mom," I finish with a chuckle.

Idaline perks up. "Well, let's go. I obviously have no responsibilities right now, which is perfect timing, and you can get the time off work, right? We don't need to do anything special. Let's just get away from here." And silently it's as if we both hear *and get away from Lila*.

I immediately feel like shit for even saying such a thing to her. "I can't take off without decent notice,

LIGHT IN THE DARK

Idaline. How about we plan a trip to the beach or something in the next few months?"

Her shoulders droop, but she nods in understanding. "At least I'm here with you."

"Exactly. Cheer up, buttercup. You could be all the way in South Carolina without Sawyer and me." I hook a finger under her chin and lift until her eyes are on mine. "Just remember, there are only two people in this world I can't live without and you're one of them. And we're both fighters. There's no way in hell we won't be together until the day we die."

Idaline smiles. "I love you."

"I love you too."

My hand slides up her thigh and rests between her legs. All it takes is a little rub and she smashes her lips to mine. Passion sizzles between us and maybe a touch of desperation. Idaline hurries to unbutton her jeans, but I slide down to the floor and help her with the undressing.

"Should we go to your room?" she asks.

After a shake of my head, I focus on making her feel as good as I know I can. We fool around on the couch for a while before moving to my bedroom to get more comfortable and take things further. Being with Idaline is like nothing I've ever experienced with anyone else. Everything is simply perfect, even when it isn't. There can be laughter, awkward moments, and searing heat and passion the next and it's all comfortable and easy. There isn't any shyness or embarrassment.

Do we need any more proof we're soulmates than that?

Afterward, just as I lift myself up on my elbows because my full weight is on her, she uses her arms to knock them out from under me.

"You don't have to do that. I like feeling your weight on me. It reminds me you're here, I'm here, and it makes me feel protected and loved, even if it is harder to breathe," she adds with a laugh.

I kiss her jaw. "Can I confess something?"

"Always."

"I know it makes sense for you to have your own place, but at the same time, I wish you lived here already. Somehow, it's harder knowing you live down the road than when you lived across the state line."

Idaline runs her hands through my hair, playing with it like that night she tried to lie to me and say she wasn't. "We'll get there," she replies softly. "We always do."

"Karen, you need to talk to her. I don't care that you don't want to get involved. She's your daughter and she's harassing me and my family. You got through to her the last time. Talk to her and tell her that she won't accomplish anything here. Hell, find out where she's staying, so the next time I call the law on her, I can tell them where she's going."

Karen is quiet for a moment and I can feel the eyes of my family on me, even though I stepped off to the side to call her. It's been a week and we came to my parents' house for dinner. Karen says the one thing to piss me the fuck off.

"You told us that you wouldn't keep Sawyer from us, that we could still see him. You haven't upheld your promise. Why should I do this for you?"

My back straightens completely and my hand turns into a fist. "What the fuck did you just say? *I've* kept you from Sawyer? When was the last time *you* called me about him? When was the last time *you* asked to see him? Don't throw that bullshit at me, Karen. You've made as much effort as Lila to see him since I moved to Raleigh. It's not my job to make sure you're in his life; that's your responsibility. You should do this for your grandson. And if not for him, for your daughter. And if not for her, because you should have some fucking decency to do the right thing here." I hang up before she can respond. She's pissed me off enough for one day and I've said all I have to say.

When I face my family again, they all avert their eyes. Everyone but Idaline. The fury in her eyes is sure to match mine. She stands, leaves my family behind, and comes over to me. She takes my hand and leads me further down the hallway. I wish she was leading me to the liquor store. The one person I thought would be willing to talk some sense into Lila isn't willing, and somehow, that's my fault.

"This needs to end. This is stressing both of us out too much. I have an idea, but I don't know if you'll like it."

Which means I won't. "What is it?"

"We sort of trap her. You hang around my apartment complex when I go home tonight, see if she shows up. Then you can follow her, find out where she's staying, and the next time she comes around you and leaves before the cops show up, we know where to direct them."

My head shakes the entire time she talks. "I'm not using you as bait for her psycho ass. No way in hell, Idaline. We'll figure something else out."

"Then you be the bait and I'll follow her."

That's not an option either. I don't want Idaline around her any more than she has to be. Idaline reads the answer in my stony gaze and huffs. She storms back down the hallway. I hurry after her and watch as she politely steals Sawyer from my father and plops down on the floor to play with him. She may be upset with me, but I'm even more in love with her. She's ready to take charge of the situation and run into it head first. Idaline's ready to grab the bull by the horns, throw that bastard to the ground, and tie him up.

I've never quite seen her like that before. There's a fierceness surrounding her, even with her pissed at me for not taking her up on one of her ideas. There's something else we can do to get this settled; I just need to figure it out.

With the tension radiating from Idaline, it seems my parents are opting to stay out of it. We've already had supper, so we're mostly hanging around and talking, up until my call with Karen. Idaline keeps Sawyer's sole focus for twenty minutes until they both seem done. Sawyer walks over to me and Idaline stands.

"I'm heading home. Thanks for inviting me over," she says to my parents. Idaline insisted on driving separately, so I had a feeling she wouldn't be staying with me tonight like she has been.

"There's no need to rush," Dad tells her.

"I actually have my first day of work tomorrow," she replies without looking at me. She didn't say a word to me about getting the job she interviewed for.

My parents congratulate her, but I am stuck on the fact that she didn't share this news with me. Why? I don't understand. Idaline walks over, plants a chaste kiss on my lips, and whispers a goodbye. I'm tempted to follow her out. One, for the simple fact of walking her to her car, and two, to ask why she didn't tell me, but something about the air around her tells me to leave her be for tonight.

Sawyer climbs into my lap, grunting all the way as if it's a huge struggle, and then rests against my chest.

"You might want to head home too, son," Dad says. "That one looks ready for bed." He points to a yawning Sawyer.

I rub his back. "You ready to go home, Sawyer? See the fish and then go to bed?" Sawyer yawns once more, which I take for a yes. "Say goodbye to PaPa and MeMa." A sure sign that he's tired? He turns his head toward my neck to hide his face as I stand up with him in my arms. Mom and Dad stand since he obviously isn't coming to them. When they ask for some sugar before he leaves, he almost reluctantly leans away just enough for them to kiss his cheek before he cuddles back into me.

There's one thing for certain: when my kid is ready for bed, he's ready and he doesn't give a shit about anything else.

By the time I get him home and into bed, I expect to have heard something from Idaline, but no luck. Should I text her? Or leave her be? Maybe she's still upset about earlier and wants some time to herself. I'll give her tonight, but tomorrow? I want some answers.

I change out of my clothes into just a pair of pajama pants and collapse onto the couch for some TV time before bed. Today seemed like a rather long day at work. This is the first time all day that I've truly relaxed.

And about five minutes later, there's a soft knock on my door. I seem to relax further, hoping it's Idaline. Maybe we can talk about why she didn't tell me about her new job. Instead, I make the stupidest mistake ever. I was so focused on the fact that it had to be Idaline that I didn't double check with the peephole.

Lila stands on the other side. Before I can say one word, she's talking. "What is it about her, FC? How is she better than me? Her name is *Idaline* for fuck's sake," she spits. "How can you love her more than me? You know I never meant to hurt you. I love you way more than she does and I can treat you better, I promise! Please give me another chance." Lila actually drops down to her knees. She wraps her arms around my legs. "C'mon, FC. We are supposed to be together. Not you and that evil bitch. I'm Sawyer's mom, not her. Let's get back together, please!"

"Get up, Lila! I don't have time for this shit." I yank her arms from around my legs and do my best to make it a gentle push away from me. "Get it through your hard fucking head that we are never getting back together. We're over. I'm with Idaline and I wouldn't leave her for you. She's who I want to be with. You're nothing but a dirty piece of shit who needs to have power over someone and we don't need that in our lives. Go back home. You're doing nothing but wasting your time and looking pathetic in the process."

All I see before I slam the door in her face is the same pissed off look I saw that night she beat the shit out of my back with the whip. I expect her to bang on the door so we can continue to argue, but nothing happens. I peer out of the peephole and it seems she's left.

Why does that worry me more than if she had stayed and argued with me some more?

CHAPTER
Nine

Idaline

I've never been so nervous before. First, I was nervous because I didn't have a job and now I'm nervous because I do have a job. I'm actually grateful to come home to my own apartment and have some time to myself as well as some peace and quiet. But between worrying about my first day and stressing over Lila, I'm pretty damn close to a nervous breakdown.

Something needs to give and I would prefer if it was the situation with Lila considering I would like to keep my new job. As long as everything goes well tomorrow, that is. I toss and turn in bed. If I'm not wondering how my first day of work goes, then I'm trying to come up with a way to get Lila out of our lives. I've reached my limit when it comes to her. She's toxic to our lives. It's obvious that when something is toxic, you get rid of it. But I have to figure out how to do so with FC's approval.

I may also feel a little guilty for not feeling guilty about keeping the news of my new job to myself. I'm just too nervous. I want to make sure everything goes well and that it looks like I won't fuck up enough to lose it so soon.

Morning comes and I'm so tired from constantly waking up from an unruly sleep. Putting on a pair of scrubs feels like putting on my favorite pair of pajamas that went missing for a long time. Who knew a simple uniform would feel more like armor than just a pair of scrubs. I actually feel a little like my old self again. Some of my anxiety fades away, but not all of it.

I'm driving to my new place of work when I get a call from FC.

"Hey," I answer.

"Hey. How are you doing this morning?"

"Good. I'm on my way to work." I pause. "I'm sorry I didn't tell you about that. I've had anxiety and I wanted to make sure it goes well first."

"Don't worry about it. I just wanted to check in on you and wish you a good first day. Call me when you get off, okay? Tell me how it goes."

"I will." Something feels off between us, but I don't have time to think about it. We have to hang up because FC is nearly to work and so am I.

My first week is going to mostly involve me sticking to a co-worker to learn the ropes of the facility, how the people operate, and always have someone nearby in case I have a question. My boss meets with me as well. He seems super nice, even with his no-nonsense attitude. I'm paired with a guy named Teddy for the day and I have a feeling

I'll like him, too. He's probably in his early thirties with a little bit of a beard, a fit body, and he's on the shorter side.

We have lunch together, which goes well too.

"Where did you work before this?" Teddy asks me.

"At a nursing home back in South Carolina. I really enjoyed it."

Teddy's eyes widen. "So, what brought you here?" He smiles. "Let me guess. Some guy?" When I nod, he laughs. "Figures. I hope things go well. You should like it here. This is a good place. The management is fantastic, the patients are mostly good to work with, and who can complain about the pay or the benefits? I think they've put you on my schedule for the first week, but everyone who works here is good people. Just be careful around Colleen and Kathy. They can be a little touchy sometimes."

Teddy fills me in on all the ins and outs of the place during the lunch, but he is back to business the moment it's over. After work, I call FC immediately to update him on my great day. My nerves about work have completely disappeared now. Unfortunately, when I get to my apartment, I spot Lila hanging around my door.

Just what I need.

"What do you want?" I hold my phone up. "I'm calling the police."

"To tell them what? There's no restraining order between us." She waits with a smirk.

"You've been asked to leave and you won't. I'm pretty sure I can call the police for that."

Lila rolls her eyes and then scrutinizes my outfit. "What are you anyway?"

LIGHT IN THE DARK

"What do you want, Lila?" I text FC that Lila is here. Maybe he can call the cops for me and by the time they get here, Lila will still be here chatting it up with me.

"I would like for you to leave FC. I want to be a mom to Sawyer. I want to be a good girlfriend to FC. We deserve another chance, but FC won't give me that as long as you're in the picture. Please, Idaline. Woman to woman, let me put my family back together."

Is she serious? She was vicious the last time I saw her and now she's all serious and sweet and talking about Sawyer. She thinks she has a family to put back together? I don't know what pisses me off more: the fact that she thinks she can be a good girlfriend to FC, or that she's trying to bring Sawyer into this when she doesn't care about him unless she can use him to her advantage like she's trying to do now.

Before I can think about the ramifications of my actions, the palm of my hand hits Lila's cheek. The slap catches her off guard. I relish in seeing her head snap to the side, her hand rising to cup her cheek, and the shock and rage on her face.

"Don't you dare say you want to be a mother to that little boy when you weren't a mother to him while you were in his life. I'm not going anywhere, Lila. I won't leave FC and I won't leave Sawyer."

Lila drops her hand from her reddened cheek. "How dare you hit me!" She raises her hand, but FC is suddenly behind me, reaching around and grabbing her wrist.

"Don't even think about it, Lila," he grinds out.

"But she hit me!"

"Go home, Lila. That's all we want from you. Please, just go home." He releases her wrist and I'm completely surprised when she steps around us, actually leaving. FC kisses my temple and whispers, "You okay, love?"

"Yeah." I release a deep breath. "I didn't mean to hit her, but she said she wanted to be a mom to Sawyer and it really pissed me off." I turn to face FC. "What kind of person is she? I could tell she was just saying that because she wanted to appeal to me and earn some sympathy."

FC smiles. "I love you."

"This is not a time to smile and tell me you love me. I hit your ex-girlfriend."

FC shrugs. "That's okay. I'm glad I was already on my way over here. Let's go inside so I can hear all about your first day."

He listens to me as I tell him all about my day while I cook dinner. And then he brings up the impending holiday: Valentine's Day.

"Don't make any plans because you have plans with me."

I laugh. "Like I have someone else to make plans with."

"I don't know. It sounded like you and Teddy were getting along pretty well today," he teases.

"He also knows I moved here for a guy. What are we going to do?"

FC wags a finger at me. "This is our first Valentine's Day. I don't plan to tell you what we'll be doing. Besides, I'm still planning it," he finishes with a laugh as he stands. "I should go home. I'm glad you had a good first day." FC comes over to kiss me. "I'll lock the door on my way out.

Come over tomorrow, okay? I'm sure Sawyer would love to see you."

"Just Sawyer?" I ask with a raised eyebrow.

He smiles. "Me too. You know I always love seeing you. Call me if you need me. Love you."

"I love you too."

FC heads out of my apartment and I watch him go. I can't wait until Valentine's Day.

Valentine's Day has finally arrived. It's been a long time since I've been excited about this holiday. I've only wanted to spend it with FC and this is the first time I'll be able to. While that makes me extremely excited, it also makes me nervous. FC must be nervous too. Imagine the pressure we're under not to fuck this up. Our very first Valentine's Day in the midst of so much stress and we'd like it to be a perfect, romantic night. A little bit of light in this dark world we're surrounded by right now.

With a deep breath, I check myself in the mirror one last time. FC hasn't told me any details about tonight. Maybe it was presumptuous of me, but I found a blue dress among my clothes. I can't even remember the last time I wore this dress. It still fits pretty well, though. After smoothing some wrinkles, I decide I'm fully comfortable and ready for whatever lies ahead tonight.

There's a knock on my door just as I walk out of my bedroom. A quick glance through the peephole shows that FC does indeed stand on the other side. I open the door and release a quick breath of relief at seeing that he's dressed up too. FC's eyes eat me up and his hands immediately grab my hips.

"You are beautiful."

I grin. "Thank you. You're pretty handsome yourself."

"Maybe we should stay in tonight."

"Nope," I quickly shut him down. "We've been waiting for this for too long."

He grabs my hands. "I know, but it was a really nice thought." FC pulls me out of my apartment, allows me to lock the door, and then leads me toward the elevator. "We'll have a nice time tonight." He takes a deep breath. "I'll do my best to stay focused on us and not check in on Sawyer, too."

By this time, we're on the elevator, heading to the ground floor. "It'll be okay if you do check in," I tell him. This is a stressful time and he's still adjusting to spending more than his normal amount of time away from his son. I won't be the one to tell him he can't call whoever is keeping him tonight to see how he's doing.

FC kisses me softly as the elevator doors part. "That's why I love you."

We catch up on our days while FC drives us to a restaurant that on the outside looks as if we're entering a old, unused building. I'm worried about our safety, too. We had to walk down an alleyway to get to the door. But the inside is beautiful. Lights are dimmed, but lit everywhere to provide enough light that it's not too dark.

We're seated at a table for two along the way with a great view of the rest of the restaurant. On the other side, the cooks are actually in full view and not hidden away.

What surprises me is that things are relatively quiet in here.

"Have I done well so far?" FC asks, bringing my attention back to him.

"Yes. How did you learn of this place?"

FC surprises me by blushing. A nice pink to dot the center of his cheeks. "My dad has brought my mom here before. He actually knows the owners."

We discuss some options of what to eat. FC is a bit more familiar, only because his dad told him what they've eaten when they've come. After we've placed our order, FC reaches across the table to hold my hand.

"How are you doing?"

"Good. Work is enjoyable. I'm having a hard time sleeping again, though. How are you?" I twist the napkin around and around my finger to keep myself occupied.

"Suspicious. Things have been quiet from Lila. She's up to something. But other than that, happy as can be thanks to you and Sawyer." He throws a smile my way. "Are you still happy you're here?"

"Of course," I answer without hesitation. "You should know that."

He shrugs as if he isn't sure. "I guess I expected your anxiety to calm down more than it has."

I can't help but laugh. "I'm sorry, FC," I begin in a soft, sweet and sincere tone. "You aren't my cure." I squeeze his hand in apology. "And this is a big change. I'll have some anxiety just because of that. Things can be absolutely perfect in this world, and I can have some anxiety over something. I'll always have some." His shoulders fall a bit. "But you help me through it and at the end of the day, that's all I need."

He cocks half a smile. "This isn't really day of love talk, you know."

"You started it," I point out. "What would you like to talk about instead?"

"How beautiful you are."

I love him. Things are still crazy and we're fighting an uphill battle, but even with the anxiety constantly flowing through my veins, peace follows. Because my one day with FC has finally arrived. My soul nestles close to FC's and we'll never have to part again. I have every reason in the world to be exceptionally happy and right now, I am.

We eat delicious food, talk about our upcoming weekend trip to visit my family, and eat dessert.

"Hey, where will we be staying while we visit?" FC asks.

"With my grandpa, if that's okay with you? He has the extra room and he asked if we would."

FC nods in agreement. I escape to the bathroom, and when I return I notice he's quiet, but pensive, and for so long that I begin to worry.

"What's wrong?"

"I've never really packed Sawyer and taken him anywhere. I'm trying to think of what I need to pack."

I laugh. "Maybe we can think about that another day. Tell me a secret."

He grins. "I've always wanted to dine and dash."

My eyes nearly pop so far out of my head they could land on his plate. "We are not, FC."

LIGHT IN THE DARK

He draws eights on the top of my hand. It lures me in as his eyes pull me closer and his soul yanks hard on mine. "Let's do it. They haven't even brought the bill yet. The waitress is so busy, she's probably forgotten about us. It's been fifteen minutes since she's even been within ten feet of our table."

"We're too old for this, FC," I chide. My heart beats erratically at the thought that FC might be even a little serious about this.

"Never!" he whispers with a mischievous glint in his eye. FC stands, pulling my hand with him, and with quiet protests from me, he drags me out of the restaurant. His grin is victorious and ridiculous as we hurry down the alleyway.

"FC, we need to go back! We didn't even leave a tip for that girl." Did we seriously just dine and dash? We are not this type of people! If we don't turn around right now, all I'll be able to think about tonight is how we didn't pay the bill and the waitress didn't get tipped. I yank hard enough on FC's arm that he stops to face me.

"What is it?"

"I can't do this. I'm not carefree enough to do this. Or whatever personality trait a person needs to do this. Why in the hell are you laughing at me?" I snap, frustrated with him.

FC cups my face and kisses my nose. "I paid the bill while you were in the bathroom. I love that you at least made it out of the restaurant." He chuckles while I glare at him. "Don't be upset with me. This was a fun little experiment."

"You're mean."

He only laughs at me, wraps an arm around my shoulders, and leads me to the car. "Let's go home for some make-up sex."

That causes me to laugh. He's already forgiven. It's no surprise either. FC can be forgiven for practically anything.

CHAPTER Ten

FC

"FC, relax," Idaline says in her most soothing tone. Her hand runs up and down my thigh as I drive us ever closer to Grandpa McAllister's house. "I don't think we forgot anything and if we did, there are stores everywhere. Sawyer's first trip away from home will be great. Don't worry."

I huff, only slightly annoyed. "Says the girl with an anxiety disorder. This whole trip is stressing me the fuck out." My eyes flick to the mirror so I can check on Sawyer in the backseat for only the billionth time. "Is his house even baby-proofed?"

Idaline squeezes my leg until I look at her. "Stop."

Just one word, but said in such a manner that I do my best to take a calming breath. "I'm worried about him," I admit. "What if he doesn't adjust well?"

She chuckles at me, which pisses me off a little. "It's only for the weekend, FC. As long as you're there and calm," she gives me a pointed look, "he'll be fine. We're getting away from home and Lila for the weekend. There's nothing to stress about."

Except the meeting the rest of her family part, but compared to everything else in life I've faced, is that really something to worry myself over? As that thought hits me, it does almost seem silly to be as concerned as I am over this weekend away with Sawyer. At least he's with me this time. He wasn't on our last visit down.

Twenty minutes later, we arrive at Grandpa McAllister's house. He's sitting in a rocking chair on his front porch and stands as we pull into his driveway. Idaline and I both get out. I focus on getting Sawyer out of his carseat. He rubs his eyes and whines. He's as ready to get out of the car as I am and he's more than likely ready for a diaper change.

"It's good to see you again, FC."

I turn to see Idaline and her grandpa standing nearby, arm in arm, with smiles on their faces. I briefly wonder if he's telling the truth. "It's good to see you too. This is my son, Sawyer."

"Hey, Sawyer," he says in a soft, tender voice. "You can call me Grandpa." He glances at me. "That okay with you?"

"Yeah. Thanks." I love that he's so easily accepting Sawyer. I feel accepted by association.

"Let's get y'all's things carried inside."

We do that, Sawyer gets a diaper change, and he hides his face in my neck as we sit on the couch. We left after both of us got off work, so it's a bit late. Definitely after Sawyer's bedtime. I rock him a little in my arms, but he's slightly interested in our new environment, too. He keeps peeking out to catch a glance at Grandpa McAllister and the room we're in.

"Your parents and I got Kelsey's old crib and brought it over for Sawyer," Grandpa McAllister tells Idaline. Kelsey is Idaline's niece, I think. "I'll keep it here for whenever y'all visit until he's old enough to sleep by himself out of it."

"Thank you, Grandpa." Idaline glances at me. "FC has been concerned about this trip since it's Sawyer's first big one away from home."

His eyes slide over to mine. "We'll make him comfortable and make sure he's taken care of. And we'll love him like he's family."

I smile and relax, as if those are the magic words I needed to hear for some reason. "Thank you."

Idaline and her grandpa talk about how the trip was down here while I rock Sawyer to sleep, not quite ready to lay him down yet. Being here, away from home and where Lila currently stalks us both, my muscles relax and I begin to feel like my old self again. How easy it is to forget how nice it feels not to be tense and on guard all the time.

This feeling right here? This is exactly how I envisioned life with Idaline. It's peaceful. That's all I've been wishing for since leaving Lila. All I want is some peace.

"FC," Idaline says softly.

I open my eyes, my first clue that I fell asleep. The others are that only one lamp remains on, Idaline is in her pajamas, and her grandpa is nowhere in sight.

"Let's go to bed."

She should've let me be. Exhaustion weighs me down like two tons of chains attached to my feet and also hanging down my back. After laying Sawyer down in the crib, I don't bother with any bedtime preparations. I shed my clothes except for my underwear and climb face first into bed next to Idaline.

When I wake up in the morning, it's to Sawyer crawling onto my chest to cuddle with me. Confusion stuns me for a moment as I take him in. He's wearing only a diaper and it's clearly morning. He always wakes up at least once during the night. And I didn't undress him when I laid him down. I rub his back and glance at Idaline who sits on the bed, watching us.

"How did he get like this?" my voice rumbles.

Her cheeks redden a bit. "He was sweating a little when he woke up around four this morning, so I left him naked after I changed his diaper. You were so dead asleep, you didn't budge when he was whining. He woke up a few minutes ago and wanted you."

"Thank you for taking care of him for me." I reach out and squeeze her hand.

She shrugs. Sawyer leaves me to crawl over to Idaline. He climbs onto her lap and snuggles against her chest just like he did me. Idaline looks surprised, but she holds him and rubs his back. I get out of bed and find some pajamas to wear, as Idaline is still dressed in hers. She lets me know her grandpa is already up and cooking breakfast. The moment I'm dressed, Sawyer is ready to come back to me.

I kiss his cheek as Idaline stands and then give her a kiss, too. "Good morning, love."

Idaline smiles. "Good morning." She wraps her arms around me. "Grandpa said my family already called, trying to come over for breakfast, but he managed to push them off until we've had time to eat, shower, and all that good stuff. I think they're pretty excited to meet Sawyer."

"I'm just chopped liver now." I tickle Sawyer's stomach, but he does this grumble and whine combo that says it's still too early to play with him.

"Pretty much," Idaline says with a laugh.

We meet Grandpa McAllister for breakfast and that goes really well. Sawyer sits in my lap while we both eat. He eyes Idaline's grandfather once more. I'm super proud of him, though, when Grandpa McAllister slowly walks over, as if treading carefully, and holds his hands out to him.

"I have a present for you. Want to come with me to get it?"

We all hold our breaths for five seconds. Slowly, Sawyer leans away from me and lifts his arms so Grandpa McAllister can pick him up. That's my boy. I watch them walk away toward the living room.

"He'll be fine," Idaline says, thinking I need reassurance.

"I know. Want some help?" She's picking up the dishes and running some water to wash them.

"No. Go ahead and shower. Everything you need is in the bathroom closet."

Leaving her, I check in on Sawyer before I take my shower. He's happily playing with his new grandpa, who got him a little toy train. After showering and after Idaline takes her shower, Sawyer runs the show until one after another her family arrives. First, her parents show up.

Her mother, Heidi, quickly shakes my hand before moving to Idaline, who holds Sawyer. I've never felt so quickly dismissed in my life. Her father, on the other hand, lags behind.

"It's nice to see you again, FC. You have a good-looking boy there."

"Thank you," I reply.

Sawyer hides in Idaline's neck, becoming shy as Heidi talks to him. When her father, Simon, speaks to him and says hello, he reaches for me. They're barely comfortable before Idaline's brother, Brandon, his wife, Candace, and their daughter, Kelsey, all arrive. Sawyer is not having any of it. With so many new people around, he's overwhelmed and shy. But Kelsey is around six years old and she's very interested in Sawyer. She stands at my knees with her stare hyper-focused on Sawyer.

"What's his name?" she asks.

"Sawyer."

"Hey, Sawyer." She waves and reaches for his hand, but Sawyer pulls it away, keeping his hand close to him. Kelsey frowns. "I wanna play, Sawyer." She spots his new train sitting on the arm of the couch next to me and picks it up. Sawyer sits up. She definitely has his attention now. "Is this his?"

"It is," I reply. "You can play with it too."

Kelsey thinks for a moment, leaning against my legs. She drives the train on my thigh and over to Sawyer's foot. He quickly reaches for it. Kelsey lets him take it. Sawyer pushes the train and then drives it toward Kelsey. And that is how their friendship begins. It's also how Sawyer slowly opens up to everyone else here.

"How's your job going?" Brandon asks Idaline.

"It's great. I think it'll work out. FC works on cars." That's how Idaline has answered almost every question she's been asked. I can't decide if it's because she doesn't want her family to focus on her or if because so far, they haven't focused on me yet. She's sitting next to me, gripping my hand in a vise, though. I wasn't expecting her to be nervous right now.

Her family is great. They accept me and take the time to learn about me as we move to the kitchen for lunch. It doesn't take long for things to seem like a regular family dinner. Idaline relaxes as well. We all know that this weekend isn't about her family spending more time with me. They were all about meeting Sawyer, who officially has a new friend in Kelsey.

That in and of itself makes this weekend a success. It almost makes me wonder if I shouldn't go ahead and put him in daycare with other kids. That is something I'll have to think about and see if I feel comfortable enough to do such a thing, especially with Lila hanging around.

"I should probably go home," Idaline says once we return to my apartment Sunday.

"Oh, no. You're staying here tonight."

She smiles. "If you insist."

"I insist."

After I put Sawyer down for a nap, we sit on the couch together. It feels good to be home. I enjoyed leaving, but I also like being home where all of Sawyer's things are. Idaline snuggles against me with her hand just above my waistline. Before I can take advantage of how close she is, my phone vibrates with a text.

I pick up my phone and see a text from an unfortunately familiar number.

Lila: *Please, FC. Come home.*
Me: *Go home, Lila. I'm not leaving Idaline. I don't want to be with you. Ever. It'll never happen.*

I toss my phone to the side. I don't know what to do anymore. She's relentless and unreasonable. I'm tired of being in contact with her, but I won't give in either. She pisses me off, too. I've worked so hard to get away from her, stay sober, and take care of my son. I've worked so hard to be happy and get to this place where I can be with Idaline. Then she comes back and tries to ruin it all.

"This won't work for me tonight, FC," Idaline declares as she grabs onto my shoulders and straddles my lap. "You're tense; I don't want to know why. I want to fix it. I want my old FC back." She slides her hands to cup my neck, interlocking her fingers. "We're together now, FC. Let's always make the most of it because it's us against the world."

That causes me to smile. "You know, I said basically the same thing to Sawyer after I mailed you my name. That it was me and him against the world."

"Now you've got me too."

My smile widens. I grab her ass. "I definitely have you. How are you going to fix me?"

Without any preamble, she removes her shirt and bra. And then she kisses the hell out of me. I'm so immersed in Idaline, nothing else exists in the world at this moment. I'm not even sure *I* exist right now. All I need is Idaline anyway. Her touch that sends my heart racing. Her kiss lights a fire that goes straight to my dick. Being with her like this, bare with nothing between us, takes my breath away. It's one of the best things to ever happen to me.

"I love you," I whisper after as we cuddle on the couch. I grab a blanket to cover us up.

"I love you," she says, kissing my chest. She lifts her head. "I'm exhausted now, though. The whole weekend and what we just did has hit me. I need sleep now."

"Whatever you want, love."

We head to bed, but a bad feeling of impending doom follows me. It keeps me up while Idaline falls asleep next to me. It follows me to work. The feeling eats away at me all day that something bad is coming. But I haven't heard from Lila, so maybe she's gone home and my sixth sense is overreacting.

Except it's not.

As I leave from work, I find a note under the windshield of my car that absolutely terrifies me and sends me driving like a madman to Idaline's apartment while repeatedly calling her.

If I can't have you, neither can she.

CHAPTER Eleven

Idaline

"Y ou bitch." I turn just in time to catch a fist to the face. Lila's eyes blaze with a fury I've yet to see. She reaches into her purse and pulls out a gun. I stop breathing. "FC won't come back to me because of you." Her hand shakes. "I'm going to get rid of you."

Oh, god. My heart launches into my throat and the world swims for a moment. "Lila, let's think about this for a second. FC definitely won't get back with you if you hurt me."

"Shut up!"

She launches toward me and my reaction is to defend myself. Lila lands another hit to my head, but with a brief moment of reprieve, I relax only because I've knocked the gun out of her hand. She either doesn't care or doesn't notice somehow. I'm backed against my door, her hands around my throat, and she rants. My hands claw at hers, but she's unforgiving in her grasp.

Giving up on that, I shove her away while stomping on her foot. She staggers backward.

"You're crazy!" I rasp.

"FC is mine! Sawyer is mine!"

I couldn't respond even if I wanted to because she comes at me again. She hits me in the nose; pain radiates, and I feel liquid sliding down my face. I mostly try to shove her away, but I do hit her in the stomach once and the face once.

"Just get away from me!" I keep shouting. "Leave me alone!" I shove her hard, hoping to put some space between us and earn some time to take a breath. With horror, I watch as she loses her footing and falls backward over the railing. I hurry to catch her, but it's too late. I lean over the edge and nearly vomit when I see her.

Lila's body is impaled on the wrought iron fence down below in the courtyard. I scurry to find my purse among this mess and immediately call 911 while rushing down to where she is.

"911, what's your emergency?"

"I...oh god...she's impaled on the fence," I blurt out as I rush down the six flights of stairs, somehow thinking that's faster than the elevator. "It's totally my fault. Oh, god."

"Ma'am. Is she still alive?"

"I'm trying to find out. We were on the sixth floor; I'm trying to get to her."

But by the time I reach Lila, a few neighbors from the complex have joined me. A man shakes his head. She's dead. I killed her. Panic swoops down and grips my heart. Blood covers her entire shirt and runs down the fence. So much blood.

The man tries to ask if I'm okay, apparently having seen the entire thing. An ambulance and cops soon swarm the complex, along with some firefighters as they work to carefully remove Lila's body. Paramedics check on me, but are only able to tell the cops what I already know. A panic attack drowns my senses.

My chest aches, my arms are numb, and I can't breathe. I hear the cops talking to the man who said he witnessed me killing Lila. Hearing him recount the details makes me want to vomit.

And then I hear, "Idaline! Idaline! Let me through!"

With wobbly legs, I stand and follow the sound of his voice. FC frantically looks around the cop who blocks his entrance until he sees me. He ducks under the yellow tape and runs to me with the officer chasing behind him.

"Are you okay? What happened?" He cups my face so gently and asks me with such concern that I burst into tears. FC stills and I can only imagine what he spots. "Is that Lila?"

I turn to see the stretcher with the white blanket over it and nod.

"Sir, you can't be back here," the officer breaks in.

"I'll leave, but she's coming with me." He holds onto me tighter.

He sighs and leaves. FC holds me in his arms without saying a word. Unfortunately, the officer left only to get his supervisor. Before he can speak, FC produces a note that was apparently left on his car from Lila. Her intent was clear. I should be in the clear because what happened was a result of self-defense, but I still have to talk to them.

By the time I'm free to go, FC is escorting me to his car.

"I'm so sorry," I tell him. "I didn't mean to. How can you and Sawyer ever forgive me?" I mean, I know Lila wasn't the best person in the world to him, but she did give birth to his child. What if Sawyer one day wants to talk to her or something and FC allows it? He no longer has that option because of me.

"You have nothing to apologize for, Idaline. It was an accident. We don't have to forgive you. You made sure you survived; that's what matters."

I shake my head in disagreement. "You didn't see her on the fence. Maybe I shouldn't have pushed her so hard. What if Sawyer asks about her and wants to meet her one day? Now he can't."

"Maybe I'm a shit human being, but I'm relieved she's gone. It means I don't have to deal with her bullshit anymore. Her stalking me and fucking with my mind. I can rest easy knowing for sure that she'll never negatively affect my son. Please, love, don't feel bad about this. It was an accident that ended her life, but she was trying to end yours."

I don't know that I can so easily dismiss it as he is. Every time my eyes close, even for the briefest of seconds, I see her on the fence.

"I was about to call you and ask why you're running so late," Nana says as we walk in. She picks up Sawyer and turns to face us. "What happened?"

"Lila's dead," FC says plainly. "She attacked Idaline and when Idaline pushed her away, she fell over the ledge outside her apartment and landed on top of a fence, which killed her on impact." He recounts the details as if they mean absolutely nothing.

Nana hands Sawyer to FC and comes to hug me. "It's okay, Idaline. You'll be all right." Her soft, sweet words cause me to break down into tears again.

"Tell her it's not her fault and she has nothing to be sorry for," FC says.

"She went through something traumatic, FC. Give her some space," Nana scolds him. "Be more sympathetic toward her."

"I feel terrible," I mumble.

"Of course you do, dear. Someone lost their life today. But it'll be okay. Maybe you should lie down and relax for a bit." She leads me to FC's bedroom and makes sure I crawl into bed and get comfortable. "If you need to talk to someone, I'm here."

"Thanks." I wipe my eyes as she leaves the room. I try to sleep. I do. Exhaustion wraps around me like a snug cocoon. But when I close my eyes, I see Lila with a pointed piece of iron poking out of her chest and blood spreading all over, her head hanging backward with eyes wide open with fear.

My fingernails constantly dig into my inner elbow. I must check to see if this is reality and not some nightmare. The pain pierces my skin each time. Eventually, I doze off, but it's not any better than being awake. My dream takes me down a worse path than reality. Lila and I argue over FC. I purposely shove her, wanting this craziness to end, and I lean over to see her screaming and clutching the iron spike piercing her through the heart.

FC grabs me by the shoulders, shaking me and yelling at me. "How could you do this? She's still important to me! She's my son's mother! You killed her! I hate you!" The more he yells, the louder Lila's screams ring in my ears.

"Idaline! Idaline!"

I bolt upright, gasping and sweating, to find a concerned FC sitting on the edge of the bed next to me. Without hesitation, he pulls me into his arms.

"You're okay."

"I don't think I am," I whisper. "I had a nightmare about what happened."

He smooths down my hair and kisses the top of my head. "When is your next therapy appointment? He will probably be more helpful than I will be, even though you know I'm here for you. Whatever you need, you tell me and I'll help you. I understand you may be feeling some justifiable emotions over what happened, but you shouldn't feel at fault for an accident that resulted from you being attacked."

What he says makes sense, but it's not working for me right this second.

"Are you hungry? You should eat something." FC stands and tugs on my hand. Reluctantly, I follow after him. "Lila's parents called me." I look at him with worry. "They admitted they were worried she might do something like this because she called them recently and she didn't sound quite right. They have no hard feelings, even though they are mourning their loss. They said they would let me know when the funeral is."

"Will you go?" I ask. It is somewhat of a relief that her parents don't blame me, but at the same time, would FC lie to make me feel better? I don't think he would, in all honesty, but I worry nonetheless.

FC sighs as he sets a plate on the table and I sit. "I don't know. I have no reason to go, except maybe for Sawyer, but even then, is that really a reason to go? Yeah, she's dead and I'm sorry for her and her family, but that doesn't change the fact that she was a shit human being." He takes a deep breath. "I have a hard time finding compassion here. I just can't with her. If that makes me a shit human being too, then oh well. I can live with that."

"So, you aren't going," I state.

He shrugs. "Doesn't sound like it, does it?"

"No. Thanks for dinner."

He nods a welcome. We're quiet while I eat. The good news is I don't have to worry about going straight to work tomorrow. I have an appointment with my therapist in the morning; talk about great timing. All I need to do is survive the night. FC doesn't say much and we actually go to bed early. He holds me in his arms, pouring all his comfort from his body to mine. His body doesn't take long to relax into a sleeping state. I, however, am terrified of falling asleep.

What if I have another dream about Lila's death? I can't stand to see her body again. I lie next to FC all night, and then on my own when he shifts away from me, with my eyes wide open. My heartbeat thrums throughout my entire body, making it hard to relax. When I hear the beginnings of Sawyer's cries, I slip out of bed to change his diaper and rock him back to sleep. There's no sense in FC waking up when I'm already awake.

My body betrays me after I lie back down and caves to the exhaustion. Instead of seeing Lila, I'm lying flat and I'm in extreme discomfort. When I look down at myself, there's a spike piercing my chest and holding me in place. Sticky blood coats my white T-shirt and my hands clutch the iron as if I can somehow remove myself. I gasp for air, but drown in blood. Two figures appear above me: FC and Lila. The spike appears to lengthen, but it's only my body sliding down as I realize they hold hands.

"You can't keep us apart now," Lila smirks. "Enjoy your well-deserved death."

Just as she turns to FC, grabs his face, and is about to kiss him, I jolt awake. I glance over to see FC walking out of his bathroom with a frown on his face.

"Another nightmare?" he asks.

"Yeah."

"I'm sorry. Maybe things will get better after therapy today. The shower is ready for you."

"Thanks." I lie in bed for a few extra minutes, though. I watch FC move around, getting dressed, and eventually going to get Sawyer who has woken up. That's when I decide it's time for my own shower.

My chest aches and my fingers tingle; good signs that my anxiety is up and running this morning. FC has breakfast on the table and helps feed Sawyer when I join them in the kitchen. Small talk is doable, but I don't really pay attention to what's going on. My anxiety annoys me enough that I take my pill that's supposed to calm me down during an attack and hope it works quickly and lasts all day.

Sitting in the waiting room for Mr. Tucker is hard. It feels as if everyone stares at me. As if everyone knows what I did. The relief I feel when I'm called to the back nearly has me floating on air. Mr. Tucker smiles when he sees me.

"How is Miss Idaline today?"

"Not that great."

His smile all but disappears. "Tell me what's going on. Have you found a job yet? Is everything going well with FC?"

"Lila died yesterday and it's because of me." Mr. Tucker's eyes widen. "She came to my apartment, pissed because she realized FC wasn't ever going to leave her and that's partially because of me, I guess. She brought a gun and started a fight. I ended up pushing her and she fell over the balcony, landing on a wrought iron fence. It killed her immediately."

"Oh my goodness," Mr. Tucker says quietly.

"I've been having some nightmares already. Some guilt. I don't know how to deal with this."

"Of course not. I can definitely help you. Now, you may not go home cured, but we'll have you better off than when you came in."

Hopefully.

But I should have more faith in Mr. Tucker. He tackles my guilt first. The part that makes me feel better almost immediately is the fact that he acknowledges I should feel some guilt because a life was lost. It means I'm human and not immune to such emotions. What I must get through my thick skull is that I'm not truly responsible. If not for Lila's actions, none of it would have happened and I was simply defending myself. The unfortunate and tragic part is the result of me defending myself.

I leave Mr. Tucker's office feeling a little less guilty and hopeful that because of that, I won't have any nightmares tonight.

CHAPTER Twelve

FC

I expect my parents and maybe even my nana to say something about my decision not to attend Lila's funeral, but no one says a word, which is relieving. I willingly explained myself to Idaline; I don't want to explain myself to anyone else again. Not only that, but it's ultimately my decision.

A week goes by. Idaline only comes by once or twice and the rest of the time, she claims she's too tired from work or anxiety to stop by. But all it is is she's still struggling with what happened to Lila. She's closed me off some, but not completely. I plan to correct this very soon. But I'm stunned when I get a call Friday after work from Lila's mom, Karen.

"How are you?" I ask after we've said hello.

"I'm doing okay. I hope you're not upset that I called, but I have something to ask."

"What is it?"

"I know my daughter wasn't good to you. I know you told my husband and me that we could see Sawyer, but Lila went a bit crazy anytime we mentioned calling you. Now that she's," she chokes up a bit, "gone, I was hoping we could come visit Sawyer."

What's sad is that I can believe Lila is what stood in the way of them being in Sawyer's life. My answer to her isn't based on anything other than my word I once gave them. "I have no problem with that, Karen. How about you come visit on Sunday?"

"We would love that. If we plan on being there around noon, is that okay?"

"That sounds fine."

We talk for only a minute or so longer before hanging up. I immediately call my parents to tell them the news. After that, I text Idaline and tell her she's spending the night at my house tonight. I don't plan on taking no for an answer. I cook dinner while Sawyer walks around and babbles almost as loud as he can. Idaline doesn't text back, which worries me until just as dinner finishes, there's a knock on the door.

Sawyer does a wobble run to the door and I follow behind. Thank all that is holy, Idaline stands on the other side. Sawyer grabs onto her scrub pants leg and tugs. She looks down at him with her exhausted, tired eyes.

"Hey, Sawyer." She bends down to pick him up. "Have you missed me? I've missed you." She kisses his cheek, earning a smile. Those beautiful eyes land on me. "Thank you for making me come over. I've missed you too."

"Well, come on in. You're just in time for dinner." I take her bag from her and drop it off in my room. When I return, we sit and begin to eat dinner. Sawyer, of course, has to throw in a few nom nom's. I decide to bring up the hard subject right off the get-go by telling her about Karen's phone call.

"That's nice that Sawyer will get another set of grandparents in his life." And then she falls silent. That won't do.

"How are you doing, love? And be honest, because I won't believe you if you say fine."

Idaline sighs. "I've been emailing Mr. Tucker a lot, so I'm still working through what happened, but the nightmares just won't go away. That's it."

Except if she hadn't said those last two words, I would've believed her. But now it sounds like she's trying to convince me that nothing else is going on.

"I'm here for you, so let me be. What else aren't you telling me?"

"I moved," she squeaks.

"What?"

"I couldn't be there." A touch of hysteria enters her voice. "I couldn't keep walking past where I pushed her or see where she died. It was too much. My lease was only a month to month, so I didn't lose out on too much money."

"How could you not tell me that? And let me help you move?"

And then she looks a bit ashamed. "Your dad helped me."

Anger begins to swish and flow throughout my body. "Why are you keeping secrets from me?" I've talked to her every day this past week. She could've told me at any point. I don't like this version of Idaline and just as I realize I'm a hypocrite, Idaline does too.

"Don't you dare talk about keeping secrets with me, FC. I waited three years to learn about all of yours. You didn't even wait a week. I'm struggling, FC. Just like you were. I was almost always understanding with you and this is how you treat me when the situation is reversed?"

My heart shatters when a tear graces her cheek. "You're right and I'm sorry. Obviously, I'm not as great being on this side of things as you were. But I want to help you and I can, and you aren't coming to me. You went to my dad, Idaline. I want you to come to me." Sawyer throws a piece of food at me with a shout which breaks the tension. "Hey, we don't do that," I tell him. He only does it when he's full and no longer wants more food.

So, I stand to remove his food from in front of him and refill his sippy cup. He's happy once more.

"I'm sorry," Idaline tells me softly. "Everything is hard right now and it's no surprise I'm not making the right choices."

"I understand that," and I do. "Just let me be there and deal with it as well."

She nods in agreement. We finish eating with small talk about her week at work and mine as well. She spends some time playing with Sawyer while I wash dishes. When I join her, I realize she still doesn't seem like her usual self. The light within her does shine a little brighter with Sawyer around, though.

"Do you really think it's okay that he'll never have the chance to meet his mother?" Idaline asks out of the blue.

"Yes," I answer with no hesitation. "Say she lived until she was old and wrinkly. The only way Sawyer would meet Lila is if he snuck behind my back and did it because I wouldn't allow it. One day, he'll have to learn the truth about Lila. The hard truth. I'll show him my scars and tell him about how long I've been sober and the struggle that's been. I would've told him straight up that under no circumstances should he meet her because she's a bad person and unworthy of him. Not to mention, he'll have you in his life.

"Now that she's dead, I don't have to worry about telling him he can't or that I don't want him to. What happened, Idaline, is no different than if she died in a car accident. That's the key word, Idaline. *Accident.* And if that doesn't help you, don't worry about Sawyer and how this will affect him because I'll handle it. Bottom line, he'll be fine."

Her gaze never wavers from Sawyer. She doesn't say anything, which concerns me, so I hope I can hit it home with one last thing.

"Lila gave birth to him. That's it. Nothing more. I'm hoping you'll be his mother."

Idaline bursts into tears so quickly and violently, she catches Sawyer off guard. He looks at her with wide eyes while I move over to pull her into my arms. She cries long and hard. Sawyer mostly stares at her, not quite sure what to make of things. Eventually he comes over and leans against my back while talking and throwing a couple of DaDas and squeals in there.

He does one that's particularly loud and it makes Idaline laugh. She lifts her head. Her eyes are red and puffy, but she's always beautiful. I wipe her wet cheeks dry.

"In case I haven't told you lately, I love you."

Those are the sweetest words I've heard all day. I grin. "I love you too."

Sawyer makes his way around to my knees. He looks between us as if waiting for us to do something. He slaps my legs a few times, giving me a big cheesy grin. I have no choice but to play with him. Idaline plays with him, too. I think the best medicine for both of us is Sawyer. Hearing his beautiful laugh and seeing him smile can lift even the lowest of spirits.

Later, I ask Idaline, "Do you want to give him his bath?"

Her eyes widen. "I don't know. He moves around a lot."

"You have to learn eventually. Come on."

She slowly follows me. We get his towel, pick out his nighttime clothes, and get the water running for him. Idaline undresses him. She flicks her gaze over to me many times and I can see her worry, but we'll conquer that. Sawyer gets in the tub. Game over. He splashes water, laughing. I flick some water at him and he loves it, too. It takes about five minutes before Idaline begins to play with him.

When I hand her shampoo, she sighs.

"What if I get it in his eyes?"

"It won't burn and he's usually pretty good. I doubt you will."

She reaches out and begins to lather his hair. My champ of a son loves having his hair washed. He tilts his hair back and grins at her. Idaline laughs.

"You like taking a bath?" she asks.

He baby talks back to her.

They both make it through bath time just fine, though Idaline scares herself when Sawyer slips and slides a few times while she washes his body. I have to remind her he's fine, and Sawyer kind of does the same thing because he laughs nearly the entire time.

Once I put Sawyer to bed, I find Idaline in my bed. It's early, but I join her. She snuggles up to my side and rests her head on my shoulder.

"How are you doing?" I can't help but ask.

"I feel a little bit better than before I came." My hand slides down to her ass, not with any outright sexual intentions, but just to move my hand and continuously touch her somewhere. Before I can say anything, she says, "Not tonight, FC. I'm not feeling that great."

"I only want to hold you. I'm glad you feel better."

"Will you just hold me until I fall asleep?"

"Of course, love."

I hold her as close as I can. There's something she wants from me. From me holding her. She's clutching my shirt as if she might fall out of my arms at any second. Or as if she wants to make sure I don't go anywhere but where I am. It takes almost an hour before her body relaxes, her breathing evens, and her fists loosen.

Almost another hour passes before I begin to drift. My mind in that hazy place between consciousness and subconsciousness.

And then Idaline jerks in her sleep. Her arms jerk. Her leg kicks out, nearly kneeing me. Flopping onto her back, she mumbles incoherently and is deathly still. She falls silent and then clutches at her chest, gasping for breath. Is this what her nightmares consist of? Her mouth opens wide. My heart hurts when I hear a quiet whine. Like she's trying to scream, but that's all she can do.

Unable to take it anymore, I shake her awake. That's almost as bad as watching her sleep. She startles awake, chest heaving, and terrified eyes wide.

"You were having a nightmare," I explain what she must already know.

Her shoulders fall. "Is it crazy to say I was hoping I wouldn't have one while I was here with you?"

I shake my head. "Of course not. Do you want to talk about it?"

"No. You go to sleep." She grabs her phone off her nightstand. "I'm going to stay up for a bit."

This doesn't sound like a good idea. I do lay down for a bit, hoping she'll fall asleep, but I fall asleep watching her reading, either something on the Internet or a book. Unfortunately, I wake up and find her in the exact same position.

"Are you talking to your therapist about your sleep and lack of it?"

She glances over at me. "I sleep."

"That's not what I asked, Idaline." I push myself up and face her.

"He knows I have nightmares."

"And that you stay up all night after you wake up from one?" I ask. Idaline sighs, which pisses me off. "You're exhausted, Idaline. How do you think that helps you overall? You've always told me that you need things to work together for you to be well. That if one thing gets out of whack, it allows for everything to follow suit and make things worse. Your sleep isn't what it should be and you've gotta be suffering because of that. It has to be affecting everything else."

"I'm handling it, FC!" she shouts at me. "Leave it the fuck alone, okay?" There's a harshness in her voice that's never been there before.

I stare at her a second before nodding. Sawyer hollers from the other room and I stand to get him. A terrifying thought hits me. Are all women like Lila? To think Idaline is anything like Lila makes me want to cringe, but her snapping at me like that sent me back to a place when I was with Lila. Little incidents like that led to the abuse with Lila. Will the same thing happen with Idaline?

The floodgates open just like that. Every horrible memory with Lila covers my mind, but so does our beginning. How I loved her at first and how we were happy in the beginning. Fear embeds itself into every inch of my skin that I'm having a repeat of that type of relationship with Idaline. She couldn't possibly be like her, could she?

I barely pay attention when Idaline emerges from my room with her bag, ready to leave. There's no protest or plea for her to stay. She gets a kiss and a send off from Sawyer and me. We eat and then I take Sawyer to my parents' house, claiming I need to run errands. All I need is some time to think. To convince myself that I'm crazy for thinking such a thing.

But the memories of my relationship with Lila are on repeat and so is the tone of Idaline's voice. My scars seem to burn and itch and be overall uncomfortable. Then I find myself at the liquor store. I stare at the tequila bottle, suddenly so damn thirsty.

This is not where I should be.

You're so damn worthless!

All I ask is that you be a man and you can't do that much.

Leave it the fuck alone!

The bottle is in my grasp and paid for within two minutes. Does this mean I'll have to break up with Idaline? I can't go through another relationship like the one I had with Lila. I can't do it. And I don't want Sawyer around it. This can't be.

Yet I'm drinking from the tequila bottle before I've taken two steps from my car.

I've never felt so conflicted in my life about everything.

CHAPTER Thirteen

Idaline

A few hours after I left FC's apartment, I get a phone call from him. There's some relief because I feel guilty over how I left this morning. But exhaustion can cause some bad reactions in people. I'm absolutely horrified when I answer the phone, though.

"Idaline," he slurs. "Tell me you won't turn into Lila. No, no, no. Promise me."

"Are you drunk?"

"I didn't mean to; I'm so sorry. Please don't beat me."

What in the hell? "I'm not going to hurt you. I'm coming over, okay? You're home, right?"

"Yeah."

I hang up and drive over there, more worried than I've been since I moved here. FC relapsed. How in the world did this happen? Why would he think I would turn into Lila? That is madness. There's not a mean bone in my body. Have I given him some kind of indicator that I would hit him and abuse him like she did?

There are three empty tequila bottles scattered on the living room floor. I find FC in the bathroom, hunched over the toilet. He lifts his head and groans when he sees me.

"Where's Sawyer?" I ask.

"At my parents'," he slurs.

I sit down on the edge of the tub. "What happened, FC? You know I'm not Lila. I'm not anything like her."

He groans again. "I don't want to talk about it."

"We need to."

He sits up and leans against the cabinet under the sink. "You were snappy and closed off this morning and it just took me back to when I was with Lila. I spiraled after that." FC shakes his head. "It terrified me to think about being in that position again."

"But you aren't," I point out. "You won't be."

"It's like your anxiety, Idaline; sometimes logic doesn't matter." He buries his face in his hands with a sigh. "Even dead, she's fucking me over."

If something like this morning could cause him to relapse so easily, I'm terrified about what that means for our future. How will he react to an actual argument? We can't have him relapsing every time. His relationship with Lila left lasting effects that could do some serious damage not only to our relationship but to him as well.

"I think you should go talk to someone," I say quietly. "This can't happen every time we have a minor argument or I get flustered with whatever is happening with my life and I take it out on you. You need help and I'm not sure we can get you through this, just the two of us."

He lifts his head and pierces me with a sad, guilty gaze. He looks broken and scared.

"I'm not going anywhere, FC," I reassure him before he can say anything. "Will you get counseling?"

"Yeah," he says with a nod. "Of course. Anything for us."

I shake my head. "No. This is for you."

"Do you hate me?" he whispers.

I slide down to sit next to him as best I can. He makes me feel better by wrapping his arms around me. "FC, I could never hate you. I'm not even disappointed. I'm worried about you and our future if we don't fix our issues."

"We'll fix everything. I promise. We're soulmates. We have to fix things and make it through this." There's a determination in his voice that makes me happy and relieved.

"Why don't we pick up, go to my apartment for a bit, and later get Sawyer?"

FC nods. I help him stand, leave him while he brushes his teeth to throw away the evidence of his drinking, and return to help him walk if he needs it. Maybe we can sober him up relatively quickly so we won't have to explain anything to his parents. I'll have to keep a good eye on him from now on too. Now that he's relapsed, there's a greater chance he'll do so again in the following weeks.

Once we arrive at my new apartment, he barely looks around. He drops onto the couch and falls asleep almost immediately. Feeling pretty exhausted myself since FC was right and I didn't sleep after I woke up from my nightmare, I go to my bedroom and lie down. I have an appointment with Mr. Tucker again on Monday and I definitely need a session. I'm beyond exhausted, absolutely worn out. The nightmares aren't going away. Now, FC has had a setback.

It almost feels like we're back at square one, waiting for that one far-off day to be happy and have all the major kinks out of our relationship. Why can't we be happy already? Why is everything so hard with FC? This is supposed to work. My soul aches for us, but seriously for FC. He's had such a hard time and apparently, I've made things harder instead of easier.

But at least I know we're both still dedicated and plan to make things work.

When things finally get to the really good times instead of only moments, I'll be much happier than I am now. Those are the times I daydream about as I do my best to fall asleep. Times when my anxiety is more manageable. Times when FC can breathe easier and not so easily fall into a relapse. Times when we're a cohesive family with Sawyer instead of me still being an outsider. Time when we can go two months without incident.

That's the dream right now.

"Idaline," FC whispers as he cuddles against me. "I feel like shit."

"You should," I reply bluntly. "I was sleeping."

"I'm sorry. About everything. I love you so much."

I roll over to face him. "I love you too."

"You add so much to my life; I don't know why I'm trying to fuck that up. But after this morning, it was like a trigger to release all those memories I locked away and I couldn't get rid of them. I'll get counseling, I promise. I want to be better equipped to deal with whatever comes our way and to make sure I can handle any other negative effects Lila left behind." He rests his forehead against mine and closes his eyes as if it's too much of a hassle to keep them open.

"You're the strongest person I know, FC. If anyone can overcome what happened, it's you."

His smile is small, but it's great to see it anyway. He kisses me. That one simple act causes me to completely relax. It's as if he's confirming what I told him: that everything will be okay. I want to fall into his kiss. Disappear into the heady sensation it gives me. Drown in the feel of his hands running over my body and the weight of him rolling on top of me.

He whispers he loves me and he doesn't know what he'd do without me. But I would know that even if he never told me because he shows me with his actions and his touch. I won't lie, though, when I say it's nice to hear it. We undress and passion, need, and desire unleashes from within us the moment our bare skin touches one another. Things move so fast and feel deliciously good that it's almost as if we come to a completely torturous stop when FC slows things down.

This seems like exactly what we need right now. This deeper connection to remind ourselves how amazing we are together, what we're fighting for, and exactly how much we love one another. Afterward, when we're lying naked above the covers, cuddling together with contentment, FC kisses my forehead.

"I'm hungry. We should probably get Sawyer, too."

"Okay."

Neither of us make a move to get up, however.

"I like your apartment," he says a few moments later.

"Thanks. I think I like it better than the old one, even before all that happened over there."

FC sits up. "I'm glad. I need to see my son, Idaline. Do you want to get ready?"

There's no way I'll say no. We get ready and head for his parents' house. About halfway there, we realize I don't have a carseat for Sawyer, but FC says we'll just borrow the one his mom has. Unfortunately, the moment his dad sees FC, he realizes something has happened. That FC doesn't look like his normal self. The remnants of his hangover show all over his face and in the way his body moves.

"What happened?" Rick asks him.

"Nothing." FC shrugs him off as he picks up Sawyer who rapidly crawls to him upon hearing the door open.

His father looks at me and then back to FC. "We aren't about to tolerate lies now, FC."

"I'm fine, Dad. I'll take care of myself and do what's necessary to make sure it's less likely to happen in the future."

"You can trust him," I say since it doesn't appear he does right now. Smiling, I add, "If you really need to worry, I'll tell you." I almost expect to get a look from FC after saying this, but I don't. He only nods in agreement.

Rick gives in. He updates FC on how Sawyer was, helps us switch the carseat to my car, and then off we go. We have a nice rest of the day with Sawyer. I hang around for a long time before heading home, just to make sure he's good and solid. I definitely won't be around tomorrow when Lila's parents come to visit Sawyer. I'm not ready for that. I don't know if I ever will be, but I know for sure that I'm not right now.

When I go to therapy Monday, the main takeaway is that when I head to my next appointment upon leaving him, I ask for something to help me sleep. I'll see my new psychiatrist for the first time and Mr. Tucker thinks that I might need something to help me sleep and tackle what he's calling night terrors. I'm not so sure how I feel about all of this, but I go along with it. We have a pretty good session and he even says that if FC calls to his office and makes an appointment, he'll get him in to see another therapist who works there.

I didn't say this to Mr. Tucker, but sleeping pills scare me. A pill that knocks me out so deeply I'm out like a light and who knows what is going on and what side effects I may endure during that time. My psychiatrist doesn't even cover the side effects, which may be for the best. I don't want to know and prematurely freak out. All she tells me is if I notice any major differences or anything that concerns me to call her immediately. That works for me.

I text FC about the news before I go to work. It should be a good week. As much as it can be with anxiety problems, sleeping issues, and relationship kinks.

"Every time I see you, you look like shit," Teddy tells me shortly after I arrive for work. "Is that man of yours keeping you up or is something serious going on?"

"Just dealing with something personal. Don't you know it's not nice to tell me I look terrible first thing when you see me?"

Teddy nods. "I know, but I can't count on your boyfriend telling you the truth. You need at least one man in your life being completely honest no matter what."

I shake my head at him. "I don't need honesty."

He shrugs and we keep on working. Maybe those sleeping pills won't be so bad. I can get more sleep and look like I'm not running on fumes. I will be sleeping over at FC's just until I'm certain I won't be having any negative side effects. We're having a date night tonight and honestly, I'm quite excited for it.

It doesn't matter what it is or what we do. But a night out sounds like exactly what we need. I work through the day before driving home for a shower and to change clothes. A nap sounds great about now, but that's not on the to-do list unfortunately. FC arrives shortly after I finish getting ready. His smile is better today, though not lighter.

He kisses me and then asks about my day as we walk to his car.

"What are we doing?" I ask.

"You'll see."

When we pull into the parking lot of a pet store I could not be more confused. FC simply takes my hand once we're out of the car and leads me inside. He leads me right to the section where cats are available for adoption.

"How can anyone have a bad day after petting cats?" he asks me with a mischievous little grin.

"We aren't adopting one, are we?" I pet a cute little black cat with wide green eyes.

FC laughs. "No. I don't think either of us are in any kind of shape to get a pet right now, but maybe once we move in together."

"Would you be very disappointed in me if I said fish are probably all I'll ever be able to handle?"

He wraps an arm around my shoulder. "No, love. Not at all. We're only here for a pick-me-up in the form of cute cats." He kisses my temple and then teases a tiny white cat by sticking his finger through the gate and letting him attempt to paw at it.

It's adorable to watch all the kittens and cats. I actually feel better twenty minutes later when we leave and I hope they all find good forever homes. Next, FC takes us to a bowling alley. Apparently, tonight is all about having fun and not thinking about any problems. That totally works for me. We're both pretty terrible at bowling, so the winner will be the best of the worst.

I somehow manage a strike. It's almost the best feeling in the world. But seeing that in this moment, FC is having just as much fun, that makes it worth the gutter ball I roll on my next turn. We need to make sure we have more nights like tonight. Nights full of more laughter and happiness. Wouldn't that be wonderful?

CHAPTER Fourteen

FC

The weather slowly warms as Idaline continues to work on the lasting effects of Lila's death and while I attend counseling. They wanted to send me to Alcoholics Anonymous, but I shut that shit down. That's not how I want to handle my recovery. One-on-one counseling works great so far and that's what I plan to stick with for all my issues.

Idaline sleeps better thanks to her sleeping pills. I'm learning how to squelch my anxieties that Lila planted. Sawyer has met his other set of grandparents and surprisingly, that hasn't turned into a shit show. They've seen him twice so far. They bring a gift each time and they play with him the entire time. They want to meet my parents the next time they come, so that's on the agenda. They always ask about Idaline, which I think is a good sign, but I don't know how long it'll take before Idaline is willing to meet them or vice versa.

We're not worrying about it too much right now. Instead, we're focusing on ourselves and our relationship. For example, tonight's date night. Sawyer is with Nana, so it's the two of us at my apartment. We've gone out a few times in the past month, but tonight, we're staying in. I have the perfect date night idea too.

"Oh, Freeley Clemeth! I'm home!" Idaline sings as she walks in.

"Don't start, love," I warn. "Or I'll scrap tonight's plan and you'll be so disappointed."

She stops halfway to the kitchen with a hearty inhale. "It smells like a fair in here."

Perfect. "It's supposed to. Come here and enjoy the feast. We have corn rolled in butter, fried oreos, cotton candy, corn dogs, and chocolate-covered bacon."

"I love you," she replies with wide eyes as she picks up some cotton candy. "Already the best date ever. Thanks, FC."

"Welcome." I sit down next to her and pick up a corn dog. "How was your visit today?" She had both therapy and a visit with her psychiatrist.

"They think I'm at a point to wean myself off of the sleeping pills. I missed a night here and there and did okay without it, so that should be a good sign. My therapist thinks that if I meet Lila's parents next time they come down to see Sawyer that maybe it will help me eliminate the guilt I still have. Otherwise, I'm mostly better."

Which is fantastic to hear. I can tell she's doing better because her attitude has improved and she doesn't seem as if the weight of the world is on her shoulders. Only a portion of it. Her eyes wait expectantly for a response on how my counseling is going since she has shared her bit. But I struggle with sharing.

For some reason, I find it difficult to talk about my visits like she does. Sometimes, she shares so much detail, and I don't want to get down to the nitty gritty like that. I don't want to be a hypocrite and tell her that I won't be talking about my counseling like she talks about her therapy visits. That's what it would make me, right? I would be a hypocrite to ask her how she's doing and then refuse to reply with full, concrete answers in return.

I've talked to my counselor about this, too. Apparently, I now have a fear of confrontation, which sounds crazy to me because I would fire back at Lila at times. So, why am I scared of that with Idaline? My brain makes no sense. But because I'm too worried about her response, I don't say anything and instead force myself to give an answer that satisfies her but is still within my comfort zone. He says I just need to tell her and that she'll be fine with it.

I don't believe him.

With a deep breath, I answer, "It's a process, you know?" She nods. Good sign. "He sometimes tells me I'm a bad patient." I expect her to laugh, but she frowns. Not a good a sign. Abort! "We're working on my issues, though."

"If you're a bad patient, then you aren't doing what he says, FC," Idaline tells me quietly. "He's only trying to help."

"I know. Whatever I don't do is because I disagree with him or don't believe he's right."

Oh, that's a really bad answer. Idaline stands angrily, the chair nearly tipping backward from the force, and she moves all the way over to the sink. Her hands ball into fists by her sides. My stupid little mind focuses on that more than anything else.

Can a person ever really, truly, without a doubt know that their spouse won't turn abusive on them? Sure, I want to say I believe Idaline never would, but how do I know *for sure?* This paranoia doesn't want to abandon me, though I desperately wish it would. My counselor says it comes down to trust.

Well, I trusted Lila.

Right?

I know I trust Idaline, but that doesn't make the paranoia go away. Seeing her fists sends me flashbacking to another pair of fists my body got too familiar with.

"FC, are you listening to me?" Idaline snaps.

Blinking, I find her walking closer to me. "Sorry," I mumble, turning toward the table. "Flare-up. Give me a second."

She immediately backs down. Any time I say I'm having a flare-up, she knows a blast from my past has distracted me, sucking me into its black hole, and threatens our existence. Idaline slowly returns to the table and sits.

"FC, can I point a few things out to you?"

I lift my head to meet her gaze and she takes that as a yes.

"You don't really talk about everything that goes on when it comes to you and your past, which is fine. I don't mind. But I'm not Lila. You know I'm not. You know that because you let me have a relationship with Sawyer. I wouldn't be in his life if you had an ounce of serious doubt that I would turn out to be anything like her. You wouldn't want me around your family and you would distance your-self from me. I don't understand what's happening, FC."

The despair and concern in her voice kills me. "Me either," I reply honestly. "I'm fine and then you do one little thing that reminds me of her and I get a rush of flash-backs and paranoia that I'll be in that same situation."

Idaline takes my hand in hers. "Then you need to stop the cycle. When I do whatever it is, remind yourself of who I am, of the facts, and do your best to stay in the pre-sent. Maybe tell me what it is I'm doing that is a trigger for you and I can try not to do it anymore."

"I'll work on it some more," I promise.

She smiles half-heartedly. "Good. Hand me some of that bacon."

And just like that, the serious tone is gone and we're back to normal. She critiques the food I've prepared as if she's some fair food expert, which she probably could be. Maybe she'll be happy when she discovers I've bought some board games suitable for two people. It's not fair games, but it's something else for us to do and have fun with.

"Sawyer will start daycare soon," I blurt out. Idaline's eyes fly to mine. "I shouldn't ask my parents and Nana to keep watching him every day. The main reason I was al-ways so hesitant was because, though the chances were slim, I was worried about Lila somehow kidnapping him. It's time now, though. I think it'll be good for him to be around other kids more and good for my family to free up their days again."

"Have you found one you like?" she asks. At least she doesn't ask if I'm nervous. Because I am.

"Mom has been putting together a list of some. She's gone and looked and talked to them, but I'm taking a day off next week to check them out myself and then see what I have to do about getting him in and if it'll be awhile. There can be waitlists sometimes."

"That's good. Do you want me to go with you?"

I smile. "You can if you want, but you don't have to take off to go. You can always take off work for when it's his first day. I'm sure I'll need someone to go with me for that."

Idaline laughs. "That little boy sure has done a number on you."

I smile, thinking of all that's changed since he entered my life. "Yeah, he's messing with my manhood."

Idaline shakes her head. "He's made you more of a man, FC," she replies seriously. "The way you care for him and worry for him and how your emotions are so easily affected because of him? That makes you more of a man than if you were stoic and emotionless."

She might have a point. I don't care either way. My son is more important than my perceived manhood.

She leans back in her seat and rubs her stomach. "I'm stuffed. What's next?"

"Board games."

"Not yet," she says with a shrug. "Let's watch a movie. And maybe sex after that. Then board games." She smiles, and I laugh. She has a good plan. That's exactly what we do, too.

Later, when we're lying in bed together, Idaline asks for a secret. Will we ever reach a point where we won't have any more secrets to share? In a way, I hope not.

That's a part of who we are and it seems like a tradition of sorts.

"I wouldn't change anything about us or how we finally got together, even though it hasn't gone as smoothly as I would've liked. What's yours?"

Her mouth opens, but she hesitates and closes it. I nudge her chin in encouragement. "Not that I'm not completely happy with how we are now, but I miss how we used write to each other."

"Then find us a pen and paper and we'll write something."

Idaline's eyes light up. A few minutes later, we're writing letters to one another. I'm still in the bedroom, but Idaline found it too weird to write next to me, so she moved to another room.

Idaline,

I wasn't really prepared to write anything today, so I'm not sure what I'll end up saying. I do think this is a great idea of yours. I've always felt I could say anything to you, but that is especially true when writing a letter. Is that true for you too? It's as if having this blank page allows for endless opportunities to write down the even the darkest of truths.

I'm sure you know all of my truths already. I love that we have that kind of relationship. I know I've told you before that I couldn't live my life without you, and that is especially true now. You help hold me up, take care of Sawyer, and constantly remind me of all the reasons for me to stay on track and work harder to be better than the day before.

I'll admit it isn't easy to stay sober. The thirst is there every day and more prominent when I'm stressed. The temptation to slip into this person I don't want to be has been strong at times. But I think about Sawyer and I think about you. That's enough to pull me through.

Thank you for moving here and thank you for being the strongest person I know. I have no doubts that I would be worse off without you. You bring so much light into my life. Sawyer has no clue yet how much he's going to love what you'll bring to his life, too. I can so clearly see our future, it's a bit scary.

Sawyer has you as a mom. Maybe you'll move in when your lease is up. Or we can find a place of our own, whatever you want. We'll get married in a few years. Maybe we'll give Sawyer a little brother or sister after that. We'll spend time together. Maybe take the kids on a little trip or two. Have a few more kids. Like five? How does that sound? Let's make a bunch of little yous and mes until we can't handle their adorable rottenness.

But there's time for that. Don't think I want to knock you up right now. The three of us still need some time alone together. I'm just saying that's our future, love. I hope you're ready for it.

Love you to the ends of the world,
FC

Just as I write my name, and feel kind of silly about it, Idaline peeks her head in.

"Done?"

"Yeah. Get back over here and let's read them."

LIGHT IN THE DARK

She takes her sweet time walking over and crawling onto the bed. Once she's settled, we exchange letters and begin to read.

FC,

Thank you. Thank you for indulging me as often as you do. Thank you for helping me through my hard times and being the one person I can always count on. I'm so happy I've moved here and despite what's happened, I wouldn't change the fact that I'm here and you no longer have to deal with Lila.

But, and I feel bad for saying this, do you wonder if we're too messed up for one another? Part of me feels like we benefit each other more, yet another part feels like maybe we're only a hindrance to ourselves and our relationship. Maybe this is all my fault because I had this idea of us all built up in my head and reality proves to be tougher on us than I ever knew possible.

There's just this little voice in the back of my mind that wants to strangle my soul. Convince it that we aren't soulmates. Convince it that my soul wraps so tightly around yours, it's killing you and causing you to suffer and vice versa. I keep thinking about how we worked so well together before I moved here and now, it's as if we can't stop the boat from sinking with all of our problems.

I love you so much, FC. Sometimes, I worry we love each other so much that we can't see that maybe we aren't good for one another. That somehow we've mistaken ourselves and cause more harm than good. I don't know why I can't get this out of my head, but maybe now that I've written it down, I can stop thinking about it and forget I ever thought it.

    Love, Idaline

CHAPTER Fifteen

Idaline

"What the fuck is this?" FC asks with confusion and hurt, clasping the letter angrily.

That was the reaction I was afraid of. Before I can respond, FC snatches his letter out of my hands.

"I write you this positive, awesome letter and you give me this shit about how we're basically toxic for each other? What the hell, Idaline? Where is this coming from? We aren't bad for one another!" he shouts as he gets out of bed to pace. He glances down at the letter, skimming those damning words. "First, you tell me moving here is the best decision and then you talk about how I apparently didn't live up to your expectations once we fucked and *then* you say, 'I keep thinking about how we worked so well together before I moved here and now, it's as if we can't stop the boat from sinking with all of our problems'? So, we don't work well together? Fucking how do we not? Damn it, Idaline!"

Why couldn't I write a letter like his? Why did I have to go and admit a fear?

"Why do you fucking think we're bad for each other?" he snaps. "After all this time, Idaline, all this time of working toward being right where we are and you're going to second guess us? Hesitate about the only thing that has ever felt right in our lives? Has *always* felt right?" He shakes his head. "I can't believe you would do this to me."

FC turns and I hurry to follow him out of the bedroom. "Wait, FC. It's not as bad as it sounds."

He whirls around and shoves the letter at my chest. "Maybe you should read what you wrote and then see if you want to say that again." He grabs his keys off the kitchen counter and walks to the door.

"Where are you going?" I holler. "You're half naked!" He's only wearing gym shorts.

"I'm going to my parents'. You should go home," he says as he walks out of the apartment, and then he slams the door behind him.

What the hell just happened?

All I wanted to do was express this fear of mine. A fear I'm pretty sure is irrational, but sometimes with my anxiety, it's hard to tell what's irrational and what isn't. How can he simply get so angry and leave? We didn't even talk about it; I got yelled out and he left. That's not what I wanted.

What do I do now? Stay? Leave? Go to my apartment? Head over to his parents' house? Freak out? That sounds like the most likely scenario.

LIGHT IN THE DARK

My stomach churns while I get ready for bed, deciding to stay put. But standing at the edge of FC's bed is as far as I get. It doesn't feel right to get in without him here. To sleep in his bed when he's so angry at me. Instead, I grab a pillow and settle on the couch. Hopefully, he'll return tonight and we can get this fixed.

Or maybe I permanently broke us?

I toss and turn all night, becoming more and more worried when FC doesn't return to his apartment. I watch TV. I read. I close my eyes and count sheep, but it's not until five in the morning when I finally doze off. Some time later, my rolling around lands me on the floor. I'm so frustrated and tired, I simply fix my pillow and stay put. What's the point?

At some point, I hear sshing and feel myself being lifted, which startles me awake.

"Moving you to my bed is all," FC tells me. "Where you should've been anyway."

"Didn't feel right," I mumble back as he lays me down.

He studies me for a moment. A long moment that feels like it might turn into something big and maybe even life-changing. But then he says, "Go back to sleep, love," and turns, walking out of the bedroom, closing the door behind him.

At least he called me love. That's a good sign, right?

I sleep for a little while longer, but awake to the sound of FC pushing his dresser away from the wall, Sawyer standing about a foot behind him. "What are you doing?" I ask. But then he stands upright again and there's a dull silver flask in his hand. I gasp as I jump out of bed and run over to him. "How long has that been there?" I snatch the flask from his grasp, feeling the weight of the liquor and his demise inside. "Have you been drinking all this time?"

The hurt that immediately passes over FC's face causes me to regret my question. His shoulders sag in defeat. "Open it," he orders quietly, the anger now gone from his tone. I do as he said. "Drink it."

My eyes widen. "I can't!" Everyone knows that alcohol and medication don't mix.

He snatches it back and takes a swig.

"FC! Why would you do that? Are you crazy?" I yell. He can't. Why? Oh my god. FC picks up Sawyer who reaches for it. This can't be happening. FC lets Sawyer take a sip. "What are you doing?" I screech as I yank the flask away from both of their hands. This doesn't make sense. Why would FC do that to Sawyer?

He wouldn't.

FC is calm as ever as he stares me down. Sawyer looks confused and pouts now that his drink is gone. I don't understand. I lift the container and sniff. Nothing. FC raises an eyebrow, daring me to drink it. With a deep breath, I take a tiny sip. "What the fuck?" I blurt out. "It's water!" Relief floods my veins, but also some fury.

"Yeah, it is," FC confirms. "Do you really think I'd let Sawyer drink tequila?"

"No, but why are you hiding water in a flask?"

"Because when the urge is really bad, I find my flask and drink from it. My eyes see a flask and my brain think it's getting tequila. The disappointment of water gives me a moment to reorient myself. Hell, at the very least, I can hold it and pretend there really is tequila in there. But there isn't. I won't fail Sawyer or you again."

He kisses Sawyer's head and then pulls something out of his pocket, causing me to notice he's dressed in jeans and a T-shirt now. My breath catches in my throat when I see a wedding band. "It's Nana's. I went to see her this morning and she gave it to me." FC's tone hardens as he drops to one knee. "Don't look at me like I can't propose right now."

"We haven't even reached a stable point yet, FC."

"Exactly," he confirms with a nod. Sawyer sits on his knee, watching this disaster unfold in front of him. "This is the perfect time. Idaline, our life isn't a fucking fairytale. It never has been and it probably won't ever be. We struggle and we work damn hard to make this work, to survive the hand life dealt us. The only reason we've made it this far is because we have one another helping support us and hold us up. This," he holds the ring higher, "doesn't mean we have to get married any time soon.

"It's a promise. A promise that we're in this until our hair grays. I'll commit to you on the worst day of my life, on the lowest day of our relationship, because I fucking love you and I don't want to walk through this life without you. I don't need sunshine and glittery unicorn shit to want to be with you or be convinced that we work together.

"And neither do you," he adds quietly, his gaze as fierce as ever. "Your anxiety won't win this battle, Idaline. And if you still aren't convinced, let me tell you about a dream I had once that still haunts me whenever I wonder if there's still a possibility that we might not stay together forever. I was still with Lila and it was soon after I found out she was pregnant, I believe. I was with her, holding her hand, and on the other side of the room was you and next to you was your soul.

"My soul left me behind to be with yours. The dread, hollowness, and overwhelming emptiness I felt still makes me sick to my stomach. We are meant to be, Idaline. You know that as good as I do. Don't you?" he asks, his voice hitching a little with worry. The ring still held high in the air.

With a steadiness I've never had before, I extend my left hand. FC's grin nearly blinds me with the happiness shining from it. He slides the ring onto my finger before standing to kiss me. It's almost like our first kiss. Knee-weakening, heart-pounding, immediately horny, falling head over heels, can't get him close enough kind of kiss.

"DaDa!" Sawyer shouts, hitting my leg for attention while adding on a few more words I can't quite make out.

FC pulls away. "I knew a good speech would pull you around."

"So why propose now?" I question with curiosity as I pick Sawyer up.

"Because it felt like the time for us and it honestly seemed more fitting to ask now than during a good time. For better or worse, love. I don't care what we're going through, what worries you have, or any other troubles. As long as you're there, things aren't quite as bad and we can survive it." He kisses my cheek and I rest my forehead against his when he pulls away.

"You're too good for me, you know."

He grins. "So are you. I'm sorry I kind of blew up on you last night, but I wasn't expecting what you wrote."

I shrug. "It's okay." I was expecting some of it anyway.

"Let's eat and do something together today. How does that sound?"

That sounds perfect. FC is more committed than yesterday and he's reminded me that I'm as committed as he is. That's what I have to remember. For better or worse, we see each other through and neither of us plans to go anywhere.

———————

My parents are thrilled and not surprised in the least when I call them about my engagement. They want me to plan a gathering so they can come up and meet the rest of FC's family. Mom also wants to know when I'm moving in with FC because "there's no sense in having your own apartment now that you're an engaged woman, Idaline."

That's something I'll have to talk to FC about. I'm a little worried about such a thing, but at the same time, I'm ready to pack my bags. After work, though, I drive over to Nana's house. Her ring is simply beautiful. It's a bit showy, but has a classic look in it. My favorite thing about it is that it came from her.

"Oh, Idaline! What a surprise. Come in, come in," she says upon opening her front door. "I see you're engaged now." She winks at me.

"Yeah, that's kind of what I'm here about."

"Oh?" she questions as I sit at her kitchen table and she worries over fixing us something to drink. "What's going on, dear?"

I glance down at this ring I adore and then up at the woman I adore even more. "Are you sure you want me to have it and wear it?"

Nana sits down, handing me a glass of tea. "Idaline, dear, of course. When FC came over that morning and was telling me about y'all's little spat and how he knew it was time to get more serious and propose, I offered him my ring before he could even get to the thought about how he needed one. I'm so happy you are part of our family and will be in FC's life. My grandson carries the name of my husband, Freeley, and unfortunately, they never met. It would be an honor to pass that down to the two of you." She sits up a little straighter. "Now, if you'd rather not accept, that is perfectly okay, too. I won't mind one bit."

"No, no," I rush to say. "I love the idea and it's an honor to wear it. I just wanted to make sure you were really sure about giving it away."

Nana pats my hand with a smile. "I'm not giving it away, dear. Simply passing it on to someone who will do justice to what it stands for just as I did. Maybe one day you can do the same."

Tears spill from the corners of my eyes. I can't help but burst from my chair and hug the old lady. "Thank you so much, Nana."

"You're welcome, my dear. I know you'll take good care of my grandson and great-grandchildren." She winks again.

I spend some time with Nana, even staying for dinner. She loves the company and I won't be one to deny her such a thing. FC calls me as I'm leaving.

"Hey. Everything okay? I usually hear from you by now and I haven't," he says as soon as I've answered.

"I was visiting with Nana and I'm just leaving. Everything is fine. How was your day at work?"

We talk about our days, which passed pretty much as normal for a bit, before I bring up my conversation with my parents.

"They want to meet your family and come up here for like a family gathering."

"That sounds nice." Yet FC sighs.

"What is it?" I ask.

"Maybe we should invite Karen and Bobby. This is essentially so everyone can get to know everyone and maybe they should meet the rest of Sawyer's family. And you." He pauses briefly. "Do you think you'd be up for that?"

Anxiety-wise, no, but I'll have do this at some point. "Sure," I reply, a little squeak in my voice giving me away.

"It'll be fine, Idaline. I'll make sure of it."

"Thanks." I take a deep breath. "There's one more thing."

"What's that?"

"Should I move in?"

FC is quiet for a little longer than my comfort would like. "Do you want to?" he finally asks. "I'd love to have you if you do."

"Only if you can promise I won't have to move again for a long, long time." This will be my third move in less than six months.

FC laughs. "That I can promise you, love."

It looks like I'm moving in with FC. It's amazing, you have to admit. All that's happened in the last twenty-four hours as a result of us simply communicating as usual, just in an old method that hadn't been used recently. Now, I have to move in and get ready for his family meeting mine. But also for me meeting Karen and Bobby.

CHAPTER Sixteen

FC

Idaline moved in about two weeks ago and things have been smooth going so far. Today, our families are meeting at my parents' for everyone to get acquainted. Idaline hasn't been able to sit down for the past hour. She's up and down, moving here and there. She's anxious about meeting Lila's parents. I haven't said anything to her yet because I don't want to make her more nervous.

Sawyer is fascinated by her, though. He can't stop watching her to see where she'll go next. It makes me wonder if he can feel her anxious energy or if he knows something is wrong. He has tried to follow her a few times, but Idaline hasn't noticed the little toddler wobbling behind her.

"I can't do it!" she blurts out. "There's too much pressure. I won't go!" And off she goes to our bedroom.

I stand and hold Sawyer's hand, allowing him to walk with me. "Idaline." That's all I say when I enter my bedroom to find her shedding her clothes. "Ahda," Sawyer repeats after me, giving me a cheeky grin. I smile back before focusing on Idaline. "Put your clothes back on. It'll be fine, love. We can't exactly show up without you."

"They'll hate me," she whispers as her shoulders sag. She finally sits on the edge of the bed.

Sawyer and I walk over to her. I sit down next to her and pick Sawyer up to sit him in my lap. "I've talked to them, Idaline. They're excited to meet you." Idaline gives me a look. "Okay, excited is a strong word, but they are looking forward to meeting the woman who will be raising their grandson with me. You got this." She doesn't say anything for a moment, so I bring out the big guns. "Do it for Sawyer, Idaline." She lifts her head to look at my son. "They are his grandparents, just like your parents are now. Do it for him. So we can be this big awkward family."

Idaline sighs. "You shouldn't be able to use him against me." She grabs her shirt and puts it on before reaching for Sawyer. "It's not fair when he's as adorable as you are."

"Whatever it takes, love. Let's go before you change your mind."

It seems everyone is eager about today because we're the last to arrive and we're still early. Everyone seems to converge on us as soon as we walk in the door.

"Everyone can back off," I say with a laugh. "There will be plenty of time to spoil my son, but you're scaring him." He's hidden his face, even though he knows everyone here. Having them standing around us, talking all at once, and various sets of arms reaching for him isn't something he's liking right now. I'm overwhelmed myself.

LIGHT IN THE DARK

They give us some room to come in and sit. Idaline sits on the arm of the chair and Sawyer doesn't make a move to leave me yet.

"Looks like y'all have gotten to know each other just fine," I say as I look at all of them. They all sort of talk at once, speaking of their excitement. Once things tamp down, I look at Lila's parents. "Karen, Bobby, this is my fiancée, Idaline."

"It's nice to meet you," Karen says. Her gaze switches back to me. "Your mom told us you were engaged. Congratulations."

"Thanks. Sawyer, son, don't you want to visit?" I ask as I set him on his feet. He looks at all the people: my parents, Nana, Lila's parents, Idaline's parents, her brother, sister-in-law, and their niece, plus Grandpa McAllister. Sawyer walks and it's like the entire room holds their breath to see who he'll go to first. For some reason, I'm not surprised when he chooses Grandpa McAllister and little Kelsey, who sits in his lap.

Conversation picks up right where it left off before we arrived. Idaline keeps squeezing my hand on and off. I actually don't blame her for being nervous still since Karen dismissed her a little. Idaline surprises me when she stands and walks over to Lila's parents.

"I just want to apologize for what happened," she begins quietly. "If I could change what happened, I would."

Bobby is the one who reaches out to hold Idaline's hand. "You were only protecting yourself; we understand that. Let's move on from it and work toward being there for Sawyer."

A simple exchange and the weight of Lila's death falls off Idaline's shoulders. It's as if I can see the weighted shroud cascade to the ground with a thud. Idaline takes a deep breath, smiles, and returns to sit with me. Whatever issues she had left? I bet this resolves them. Her soul is much lighter. I can see it and feel it.

With that over, the rest of the evening goes well. All of the grandparents get to know one another and spend some time spoiling Sawyer. Karen and Bobby get to know more about Idaline, too. The most surprising and disturbing turn of events is the flirting going on between Nana and Grandpa McAllister. Idaline seems to be stunned into disbelief.

"He hasn't flirted like that with anyone. What is happening?" she whispers.

"Let them have their fun."

It is a little weird, though. After eating, Sawyer is ready for a nap. Karen and Bobby head home since they have quite a drive. Idaline's parents are next to go once Sawyer has fallen asleep in Idaline's arms. I'm actually in no rush to head home, but maybe I should be. We're sitting on the couch, talking, and Idaline's head falls onto my shoulder. Sawyer isn't the only one who's tired.

"Maybe you should get your family home," Nana says.

"Trying to get rid of me, Nana?" I ask.

"Not really, but I'm heading home."

I offer to stand to hug her goodbye, but she doesn't want me to disturb Idaline, which is funny considering she wants me to wake her so we can go home. I wait another thirty minutes before waking her and dragging her home.

"How do you feel about today?" I ask as I drive us home.

"Good. I'm glad everyone seemed to get along and that Karen and Bobby don't seem to hate me."

"I told you they wouldn't," I can't help but point out with a smile.

"I know, but it's good to know for sure, you know?"

"Right. Now you have that hurdle over, too. No more anxiety when it comes to seeing them or worrying about not being here to avoid them. We can all move on."

"That sounds nice. It feels like we can put our past officially behind us now, doesn't it?" she asks with a quiet sign of hope in her voice.

"Yeah, I think so." To have everyone together like they were today? Happily getting along and acting like a family? It's as if our pasts aren't running our future even a tiny bit anymore and we're firmly in the present and heading for a fun future.

Wow.

What a nice feeling. It's unusual. It's been so long since I've felt this. Since I was confident that my past wouldn't rear its ugly head and ruin everything completely; that I could stuff my past away and not worry about it because even if there's a flare-up, it'll be temporary and manageable.

"Have I told you today that I love you?" I ask as I pull into my parking space.

Idaline looks over at me. "Maybe once or twice."

"Not nearly enough." I lean over to kiss her softly. "I love you."

"I love you too."

"I can't do it, damn it!" Frustrated, I toss my cup into the sink. "I'm not strong enough."

Today is the big day. Sawyer is supposed to start day-care and I'm having some serious anxiety. We haven't even left the house yet. The idea of leaving Sawyer in the hands of non-family members stresses me out with every second that passes.

"What were we thinking anyway? This is a stupid fucking idea. We can't leave him in the hands of people who have no vested interest in keeping him alive."

Idaline's hand rests on my back. "FC, you're freaking out. This will be good for Sawyer. He'll make friends and interact with kids his age."

My head falls. "I don't know if I can do this."

She steps away and a moment later a small hand touches my arm. "You have to do it for him. Let's go." Idaline then walks away with Sawyer. I follow her because with this stress, there's no way my son is leaving my sight right now.

Idaline is my rock. She drives us there to allow me to sit in the back with Sawyer, who is thrilled to have company. When we arrive, the only reason I get out is because Idaline takes Sawyer out of his carseat and I follow along.

We meet the lady who gave us the tour of the daycare center, Mrs. Boulder. She smiles wide and radiates with energy.

"Mr. Hart! It's so good to see you. This must be little Sawyer. Are you excited about your first day?" she asks

Sawyer, who completely ignores her, his eyes on all the little kids behind her.

"I'm not so sure about this," I admit to her.

She smiles warmly at me. "First day jitters are completely normal. You're welcome to stay for a few minutes with Sawyer and to do two five-minute video chats with us, but for Sawyer's sake, we only recommend staying for a few minutes. We'll keep you posted on anything serious, but your son is in good hands, Mr. Hart."

"He won't be staying," Idaline answers, causing my head to snap over at her. She lands a firm gaze at me. "It will only be harder on you. He will obviously be fine." Sawyer is wiggling like crazy in her arms, dying to get down and he's two seconds away from crying in anger from being prevented. "Say goodbye."

If it's possible to hate Idaline, I do right now. Regardless, I kiss my son, tell him I love him, and then watch Mrs. Boulder take him away. Sawyer is tickled to death and fascinated to be around other kids. He watches at first, but a little boy walks up to him and hands him a block. His second friendship, if we count Kelsey as his first. My heart is all warm and fuzzy and ready to burst.

Idaline wraps her arms around my waist. "See? He's having fun already."

"He doesn't even care that we're leaving him."

"Our little boy is growing up," she whispers.

And then my heart explodes because she called Sawyer *our boy*. Idaline has accepted Sawyer as hers and I couldn't be happier. It's definitely time to work on getting those adoption papers prepared.

"Let's go before we stand here all day. I don't want to be late for work." She turns us around and we leave with Sawyer being none the wiser.

Unfortunately, it takes everything for me to not return to the daycare to pick him up throughout the day. The good news is that whenever I have that thought, I can pull up a website on my phone. One reason I liked this daycare is that they have a webcam continuously running and parents can tune in on their website to see what their child is doing at any moment.

Sawyer seems to be having a blast every time I tune in. He's playing with others, but sometimes, he's playing alone. All I care about is that he looks happy and unharmed. The work day seems to pass slowly as I wait for the time when I can pick him up. When I finally get there, Sawyer spots me after a moment and comes wobbling over as fast as he can, giggling with a big smile on his face.

I don't think he's ever been so happy to see me. I can get used to a greeting like this. I pick him up and kiss his cheek. "Hey, son. Did you miss me?"

"DaDa!"

I laugh. "I missed you too." Once I get him checked out, we head to the house to get started on supper. I should finish just in time for when Idaline gets home. Sawyer seems to babble more than usual, but he falls asleep on the couch before Idaline can get home. I guess daycare wears him out.

"How did today go?" Idaline asks as soon as she walks in the door.

"He's asleep on the couch, so it must have been too exciting to stay up for dinner." As soon as I say this, she turns around and walks to the couch, peering over the back of it.

"Aw, he's adorable. He looks like he's sleeping so good."

"I think I'll let him sleep for a while and feed him when he gets up. Get over here and kiss me so we can eat."

She laughs. "Yes, sir."

This is the best ending to a workday that I could imagine. I'm sure our future will include many more of them.

Epilogue

FC

"**D**eclan, if you fall out of that tree again, I won't take you to the hospital!" Idaline hollers to our ten-year-old son who has a knack for being both adventurous and clumsy.

He laughs and shouts back, "Yes, you will!" Sawyer, now fourteen, chases our two youngest daughters, Ashley and Corrine, five and three, around the yard. They absolutely adore him and thankfully, he doesn't mind entertaining them every so often. Lastly, our eight-year-old son, Vincent, sits on the other side of Idaline on the bench. He has trouble in school and hasn't finished his homework yet. Idaline has told him three times he could play with his siblings, but he's determined to finish what he's started.

I have no fucking clue how I ended up with five children from fourteen to three and married to my soulmate. Our house is constantly chaotic, but Idaline handles things surprisingly well. She takes time to herself when she needs it and I double-check on her sometimes to make sure she's taking care of herself, but she's more amazing than ever.

"Love?" Idaline looks up at me with a lazy smile. "Want to cross another name off your list?"

She laughs and playfully pushes me away. "We'll never cross them all off, FC. There were at least a hundred names up there and we've used ten of them already. Go play, buddy," she finishes to Vincent. Once he's gone, she faces me fully, still smiling. "Five isn't enough for you?"

"Five is plenty, but we're uneven, Idaline." I rest my hand on her stomach. "Plus, I love seeing you pregnant."

She plucks my hand off her stomach. "All I hear is caveman talk for I love having a mini me inside you."

I laugh heartily as Sawyer walks up to the picnic table.

"What are y'all talking about?" he asks skeptically. "You aren't pregnant, are you, Mom?" His gaze bounces between the two of us. "No! I can't handle more of these rugrats! I'm exhausted." Sawyer lays out all dramatic-like over the table with his hand over his forehead. "I mean, another brother or sister would be cool, but for the love of god, lay off! Aren't you old people tired yet?"

"Sawyer, stop it," Idaline orders with a bit of a chuckle. "I'm not pregnant. Our family is complete." She gives me a pointed look that's serious enough for me to know that she doesn't want more kids. I should know this already because she's made mention of me going to the doctor for a vasectomy. This was my last attempt to change her mind.

Sawyer sits up and looks out at his siblings playing. "So, this is it, huh?"

"This is our family," she confirms.

"Do we have to tell them about me?" he asks with a serious tone in his voice.

Sawyer recently learned about Lila. Having three sets of grandparents around was bound to bring up questions sooner or later, and he finally asked why he had so many when other kids don't. That wasn't a fun discussion and Sawyer is still processing what we told him.

That Idaline isn't his biological mom, but she's been with me and raising him since he was one. That she adopted him before he turned two. That my scars are from his biological mom and that she died in an accident while attacking Idaline. It took us almost as long to decide exactly what to share as it did to tell him. But we didn't want him to later feel like we held out on him or lied, so we told him the bare bones and answered any questions he asked.

"Sawyer, there's nothing to tell," Idaline replies softly, reaching to cover his hand with hers. "You are still their brother and our son."

He turns to face us and my heart cracks at seeing his eyes watery. "But I'm not like them. I have a different mom and she was mean."

"No." My tone is so strong that his head snaps over to me. "You're exactly like them. Someone else gave birth to you, Sawyer. That's it. You're otherwise exactly like them. Nothing has changed. Do you hear me? We're all the same. We're all a part of the same family. Hell, you basically have Idaline to thank for your name."

Sawyer frowns. "What do you mean?"

"We were best friends while he was with Lila," Idaline says. "He came to see me once and I showed him a list of my favorite names for my future children. He stole," she gives me a playful smile, "Sawyer and Nash from my list to name you." Idaline stands to hug Sawyer. "You're ours, sweetie. You only know more of your history now; that's it." Her voice lowers just a bit, but I can still hear her. "And to tell you the truth, you're my favorite." She pulls away with a wink.

Sawyer laughs. "Thanks, Mom. I kinda figured that."

"Sawyer! Help! I'm stuck!" And that's Declan, who apparently can't figure out a way down from the tree. While he loves to climb trees, he always has trouble getting down.

"I'll get him," I tell them. "You sit here with your mom and think about all your good memories with her."

"Dad, where's Sawyer?" Declan pouts. "You're too old to climb trees."

"Don't bite the hand that feeds you, son," I tell him as I begin to climb the tree.

"See? That's what old people say." Did I also mention that he's our adorable smart mouth of the family?

I start to regret my decision when I reach Declan, who is nearly at the top of the tree. The branches creak and groan underneath my weight. I might not be too old to climb a tree, but I might weigh too much.

"All right, Declan. Arms around my neck and legs around my waist."

After a few minutes of helping him over and securing him on me, we begin our descent. We're halfway there when the branch snaps and I lose my hold on the other. Declan screams bloody murder in my ear. He holds on tight to my neck, but his legs fall from my waist.

And then everything goes black.

"Call 911, Sawyer! FC! Come on, FC. Wake up."

I open my eyes to see six faces peering at me and a shit ton of pain radiating in my head. Idaline has tears falling down her face, but I don't understand why.

"What's wrong?" I ask. "Why is everyone looking at me?"

"Ambulance is on the way," Sawyer says.

"Why?" I ask.

Idaline frowns. "You fell out of the tree, FC. You went up to get Declan and y'all fell. You hit your head pretty hard when you landed."

My eyes find Declan. "You okay, son?"

He nods. "I'm sorry, Dad." His voice cracks.

"It's okay. I'm fine."

"But you aren't getting up."

Right. I'm still laying down. My hands find the warm grass and I push myself up. Idaline protests, but I'll be fine. My kids need to see I'm okay. Even though my vision swims a little and Idaline places a hand on my back to steady me. "See? A-OK, kids. Just a little bump on the noggin'. Dad will be okay."

Corrine crawls onto my lap and cuddles against my chest.

"You scared us," Idaline says what they all seem to be thinking.

"It'll take more than falling out of a tree to bring me down. Go pack up what you'll need to carry everyone to the hospital. Sawyer can stay here with me until the ambulance gets here."

LIGHT IN THE DARK

She looks like she wants to hesitate, but it hits her what I said. That I'll definitely be going to the hospital. Idaline rounds up the kids and takes them inside with her. Sawyer and I sit quietly next to one another until the ambulance arrives.

"Can I ride with you, Dad?"

"I'll be fine. Go with your mom. Help keep her calm and look after your brothers and sisters." Sawyer opens his mouth to object. "You've seen her when she's worried, right? But you've never seen her when she's worried about me. Go help your mom and look after her for me. I'm okay. Just need to get checked out."

He nods and off I go to the hospital. Unfortunately, they diagnose me with a concussion. When the doctors are done, I expect Idaline to waltz in at any minute, and I start to worry when she doesn't. I really worry when Sawyer walks in with the rest of his siblings lagging behind him.

"Where's Mom?" I ask. All of their faces are pale and scared. "Where's Mom?" I repeat, while pressing a button for a nurse.

"I don't know," Sawyer answers. "She was getting antsy waiting and then I don't know what happened, but doctors came and took her away on a stretcher. They wouldn't tell me anything."

"NURSE!" I shout. Pain pierces my skull, but it's worth it because a nurse rushes into the room. "Where is my wife?"

"Your wife?" she parrots.

"Yes, my fucking wife. Where is she? My kids say doctors took her on a stretcher while they were waiting on me. I need to know what the fuck is happening with my wife."

"Okay, okay. What's her name?"

"Idaline. Idaline Hart."

She scurries off to find out what we all need to know. The kids are all huddled together, looking worried sick.

"Come here. Everything is okay. I'm fine. I hurt my head, but I'll be better soon. It's nothing serious."

Sawyer sets Corrine and Ashley on the bed with me. He stands while Declan and Vincent sit on the edge down by my feet.

"Mom will be okay too." I hope I'm telling the truth, considering I don't have the faintest idea what happened out there. We sit there, waiting in silence for what feels like forever. My girls fall asleep on me. Poor little Vincent won't say a word. He's a momma's boy for sure. He looks the most worried out of everyone, if that's possible.

The nurse finally returns. "Mr. Hart, your wife is being examined. She wasn't feeling well while she was waiting and she fainted. They are just looking her over to make sure she's okay and that it wasn't anything more than stress."

"When will I be discharged?"

"They are working on your papers right now."

"Can I go see her?"

She looks over my children. "It may be best if you stay here with your kids."

"What about me?" Sawyer asks. Declan and Vincent look at her hopefully, already planning to tag along I'm sure.

The nurse flicks her eyes over to me. "Mrs. Hart didn't ask to see anyone."

All of my boys' shoulders fall. I'm not about to leave Idaline somewhere in the hospital. They apparently want me to stay put, so, "Show them where their mother is."

"I really don't think—"

"It's either all of us, or only three of us. Your choice."

She sighs, but leads the way for my boys.

The only thing left for me to do now is wait to be discharged and for news on Idaline. My discharge comes first. That leaves me carrying the sleeping girls to where Idaline waits. I hear her voice before I see her. Hear her laughter. That alone relaxes me completely. Whatever is going on, we'll all be okay.

When I see her and my boys, they are all smiling.

"Hey," Idaline says. "What happened with you?"

"You first."

"Mom's pregnant," Sawyer says with a shake of his head and a small smile. "Looks like we're not quite complete after all."

I stare at her as if I've never received that news before. It's the same every time with Idaline. I hear we're having a baby and I can't quite believe that we're being blessed with another baby. Idaline laughs and wiggles a finger at me.

"This is the last one, FC. I mean it." I nod in understanding. I'll have to schedule a procedure here soon; that's her underlying message. "Now, what's going on with you?"

"Concussion. When do you get out of here?"

"They are in the process of discharging me now. Are you okay?"

I walk over, shooing kids out of my way as I go. "I'm fine. Are you?" She was pretty assertive just a few hours ago that she didn't want another baby and now we're getting one.

Idaline nods with a smile. "I'm okay. It feels right. It feels like we're supposed to have one more. I'm excited."

"Come kiss me."

She leans forward despite the groans from our children. "I love you, FC."

"I love you too, Idaline. More if you'll go ahead and kiss me."

She laughs and does just that. Our life is about to get crazier, but even better. Thank god for this woman and these children. I'd be lost without all of them. But I won't have to worry about that because Idaline's here for better or for worse and well, my kids couldn't get rid of me even if they wanted to. This is most definitely a life full of so much light and I wouldn't change a thing about it.

If you are in a domestic violence situation and would like to reach out for help, consider family, friends, or the National Domestic Violence Hotline (http://www.thehotline.org/).

You can also call them at 1-800-799-7233

Next up is Collin Kessy's book in
the *Carolina Rebels* series.

Check Lindsay's website and social media for updates!

Acknowledgments

Thank you, Kristalyn Thornock. It's been too long since I've seen you and we must plan a get-together ASAP!

Thank you, Angie Wells, for being a beta reader for me! Your feedback is much appreciated!

Thank you, Shannon Page, for editing my work and for being so fantastic to work with.

Thank you, Robin from Wicked by Design, for creating two absolutely beautiful, perfect covers for this duet.

Thank you, Julie from JT Formatting. I would flail without you!

Thank you, reader, for taking the time to read this story. I hope you love it as much as I do.

L indsay Paige is the author of multiple Young Adult, New Adult, and Sports romances. She also enjoys writing books with characters who deal with anxiety and depression, issues which are close to her heart. Lindsay is a North Carolinian who loves watching hockey, sharing puns, having conversations with her min- iature Schnauzer, re-watching episodes of M*A*S*H, and living her dream of writing books for a living.

If you would like to hear news before anyone else, interact with Lindsay, and have a place to discuss her books with fellow fans, join Lindsay's League on Facebook.

Author Links:

Website: www.lindsaypaige.com

Facebook: http://bit.ly/LindsayP_FB

Facebook Group: http://bit.ly/LindsaysLeague

Instagram: http://bit.ly/LP_Insta

Lindsay has written the following books/series:

Bending Under Pressure

Bold as Love series

Bracing for Love series

Carolina Rebels series

Don't Panic

Hearts in Carolina series

Heaven and Hell Duet

Sanity series

Without a Doubt

You Before Me

She has cowritten the following series:

The Penalty Kill Trilogy

Oh Captain, My Captain series

The Ninth Inning series